D0347992

Heðin Brú

The Old Man and His Sons

Translated from the Faroese by
John F. West

TELEGRAM

First published in 1970 by Paul S. Eriksson, Inc., New York, USA

This edition published by Telegram in 2011

ISBN: 978-1-84659-073-3

© The Literary Trustee of Heðin Brú, 1970 and 2011
Translation © The Literary Trustee of John F. West, 1970 and 2011

A full CIP record for this book is available from the British Library.

Printed and bound by Thomson Press Ltd (India)

TELEGRAM
26 Westbourne Grove, London W2 5RH
www.telegrambooks.com

ACKNOWLEDGEMENTS

The translator would like to express his gratitude to all the Danes and Faroemen who have helped him in preparing this translation and the introduction. In particular, he would like to thank Professor Christian Matras, Hr Róland W. Høgnesen, and Hr Hanus Andreassen. Most of all, however, he is indebted for the kind help of the Danish translator, Hr Povl Skårup, who has been always ready with prompt help over the difficult idiomatic and colloquial expressions with which the Faroese language abounds. Any errors are, however, the responsibility of the translator alone.

CHAPTER ONE

A school of blackfish is in Seyrvágs Fjord – two or three hundred small whales, swimming silently round in little groups, and longing to be back in the broad ocean again, for this is not the way they intended to go. Man has turned them aside from deep-sea voyaging, to pen them into these narrow waters.

In Seyrvágur everyone is on the move. Tooting cars, packed with men from the other side of the island, come nosing their way in through the village streets. Fully manned boats come thrashing through the fjord to set folk ashore. Every mountain track is alive with men hurrying down to Seyrvágur. And so people flock in from every direction, crowding the village. Every courtyard is packed. The crowd surges through the street, down to the quayside and into the boats – a vast, bustling throng of whale hunters.

Over here, you can see sturdy old men clad from head to foot in their thick homespun, their heavy whaling knives at their belts. These are the men who grew up at the oar, and trod out the mountain paths. For them, all journeys were long journeys and risky ones. They are all keyed up to meet any problem, and they take life very seriously. These men stride onwards with ponderous footsteps – strong men of few words.

And over here, you can see the young fellows dressed in their sweaters and overalls, with their cloth caps on their heads. They have simply come along as they were, because they were only going whale driving in Seyrvágs Fjord. These are the men who built the roads and the landing stages, who learned to deck in their fishing boats and install motors in them. They measure time and distance differently from the older folk. Journeys are shorter for them, and time is not such a serious matter. These men are lighter-footed, lighter-hearted, and more lively-spirited than the older people.

In Seyrvágur village every door is flung wide open, and friendly, smiling villagers stand on their stairways inviting everyone inside. 'Don't stand out there, now, come along in and have a bite to eat!' they say. And the limited house-room is soon full, though there is still plenty of room in their friendly hearts.

That morning, when the alarm was given summoning everyone to the whale drive, Ketil and his son Kálvur were mowing their hay in the meadow near the village. The instant they heard the shouting, they threw down their scythes and hurried home. Taxis were already starting up, and the motorboats were throbbing away at the quayside. But Ketil thought they ought to walk. 'We don't save up our money to go joy-riding,' he said. Kálvur didn't care to walk over the mountains, but Ketil tried to talk him around into it. 'It's stupid, wanting to spend your money on taxis.' He measured down his leg with his hand, and then stretched his hands out sideways. 'If we keep the money and buy whale meat with it,' he said, 'we'd get a piece as big as that!' This convinced Kálvur, and he agreed to walk.

They fully equipped themselves. They took along a whale-hook, a harpoon, a length of rope, a casting-stone and a whalespear, and set off.

'Look how fast the taxis are driving, Father,' said Kálvur enviously, trudging along, bent under his burden.

'Just think of that big piece of meat, my lad, and don't grumble. We'll get to Seyrvágur soon enough. Dogged does it. Now, take it easy up the hill as far as the pass. There's no hurry. No need to go twenty to the dozen on the way to a Seyrvágur whale drive.'

Kálvur stubbed his toes on a stone. 'Wouldn't it be better to go along the road, Father?' he asked.

But Ketil did not care to do that. 'The old fell-track has been good enough all my lifetime, so it'll be good enough today.'

Kálvur did not reply, and they trudged determinedly onwards. Ketil panted, and moaned, 'God grant we make a whale-killing, that's all I pray! Now I can't move another inch – not a step – I'm swimming in sweat! But if only we get them ashore! Ah, well, this'll be my last whale hunt, I think.'

And the old man struggled on, moaning as he clambered over the fellside, but determined to win through.

They reached Seyrvágur and walked down to the quay, where a boat was just ready to cast off. 'Can we come along with you?' asked the old man.

'Of course, come aboard.'

So they slung their gear into the boat and began to lend a hand.

Just as they stepped into the boat, there was a flurry of activity and a babble of voices back in the village. An excited crowd came down to the boat-houses, led by one of the hunt foremen, a handsome, broad-shouldered fellow from Seyrvágur. In one hand he held a harpoon, and in the other a leg of dried mutton. He walked with long, swift strides – a man of much responsibility, now entering on his task. Now he had to show what he was capable of, both as a hunt foreman and as a Seyrvágur man. So he leapt into his boat and hurriedly pushed off. 'Off we go, then!' he called out.

The mass of boats moved forward. Motors throbbed, oarlocks creaked, and sails swelled to the breeze. And the whole fleet set out to the hunt.

Ketil and Kálvur were aboard a medium-sized row-boat called *The Troll*. The old man was quite out of breath after the walk, and asked the crew to excuse him from rowing. They gladly agreed. Then he sat in the stern, and spat out over the water towards the next boat. He added, 'You'd better put me ashore when we come to Tindhólmur. I'm not very much use in a whale hunt any more. But if a whale comes my way on the shore, I expect I should be able to deal with it.'

'Yes, we'll put you ashore there,' said the men. One of them asked him for a chew of tobacco.

'Of course, of course,' he replied, rummaging in his waistcoat pocket. 'On a whale hunt, the tobacco always goes round, that goes without saying.'

The men were discussing the prospects of making a kill. Kálvur simply sat listening to what was said, but he did not join in. If he was spoken to, he would mumble a reply, hang his head, and blush. He very much wanted to know just where the whales were, but he did not dare to ask, for fear of looking foolish. For perhaps it was a thing everyone ought to know in advance, or perhaps it was silly to ask where they were, as if they weren't in the same place every time. No, it was better to be careful and say nothing in front of strangers, for if he asked anything silly, they might make fun of him. He could just imagine how they would answer him.

'The whales are in Seyrvágs Fjord,' they would say.

'I know that, but whereabouts in Seyrvágs Fjord?'

'In the water!' And then they would all have a good old laugh at him. Or someone might answer, 'Oh, no, they're up in the village. The biggest one's taking it easy in an armchair by the boathouses near Ólavsstova!'

And Kálvur was horrified at the idea that he, a stranger, might be so treated. 'I would rather they had not let me in their boat at all. Then I might have joined up with someone better than this rascally crowd,' he thought.

The whales were swimming quietly around, some way off Selvík, when the boats approached them. The District Sheriff now sailed out to these people he was commanding for the day, then turned about, and all the boats drew up in a crescent to begin the drive.

The whales would lie quiet for a time, side by side, with their black heads sticking straight up out of the water. Then they would sink for a bit, come up to blow, and sink once again. It was like this the whole time. Sometimes they would shake themselves a little, and rub one against another. Then their skins would squeak together, and the old men would turn their heads, striving to catch the promising sound from this great harvest that had come to them from the ever bountiful sea.

Slowly, the hunters pulled up toward the whales. In every man's hand was a casting-stone – a simple implement consisting of a stone three or four inches across, firmly secured to a length of fishing-line. As soon as they were near enough, the hunters splashed the water vigorously. The whales swerved round, threw up their tail fins and dived. The boats paused. No one knew exactly where the whales would reappear. But then they came in sight again, right out toward Múli headland, still moving. The boats were left far behind, as the whales carried on with the same speed right toward the little bay at Tindhólmur, so fast that no one could keep up with them. When the whales realised that land was ahead of them, they veered slowly around again. But now the boats were ahead of them, barring their way. So they turned and swam right along past the low cliff of the island. The people on the shore stood gazing at them. It was magnificent to see how splendidly the whales came streaking forward, the whole school tight together, with a single course and a single velocity.

Now their heads would appear, and you would hear the whales blowing; their dorsal fins would cleave the surface of the water, and you would see the full length of their bodies. Then, with a bubbling noise, the water would surge around their heads, and they would be lost to sight, all except the light blue streaks left by their side fins. So sure was their course that it seemed as though they had forgotten the narrow space into which they were confined, and unhindered were once again shaping their course through the vastness of the ocean. But now they came to the rocks by the coast, so they would have to turn westward, past the skerries. But here, too, there were boats, and the whales turned around and went back once again.

Now one boat went forward to the whale flock, to begin the kill. A man stood up in it, making his way to the prow. He raised his whalespear, and plunged it down into the water. The hindmost whale leapt forward, wounded, and, trailing a thick stream of blood, pressed sharply into the back of the flock. This made the other whales panic, and they rushed in toward the land. But around the coast of Tindhólmur there is no sand onto which the whales can be beached. There are rocks by the shore, and the whales turned back to sea again. So all the boats now came forward, and their crews made free with their spears.

Meanwhile, Ketil was sitting on a mound looking on. He was in a high state of excitement – his eyes were bulging and he was waving his arms about. Every time the whales moved toward the bay, he took heart. 'Yes, yes, the Lord is going to be bountiful to us! Strike, now, strike! Where's *The Troll?* Why aren't they coming forward to help the kill, when it's all going so well?' Just at this moment, the first blow was struck. 'Get at them now! Every man with his spear!' he shouted, waving his arms excitedly and stamping his feet. When he saw the blood stream out, he called out, 'Well done, well done! Those fellows are nearly all from Vestmannahavn,' he added. 'They should always send in the Vestmannahavn men first, because they know how to handle their spears better than anyone else.' And he became so excited that he threw himself down on the sward and started pulling up bits of turf. But if the whales should turn toward the sea for a moment, he would start to lose courage, and pray every good power for help, lest the whales should slip away back to sea and this rich harvest of meat be lost.

The whales swam around in ever-diminishing circles among the boats, while more and more of them were speared and trailed thick streams of blood behind them. By degrees, the water reddened, and the sand and mud were stirred up from the sea bed, so that before long the whales had lost all sense of direction, and were swimming aimlessly hither and thither, each one his own way. The hunters were soaked in sweat, but still they struck at the whales. The more blood there was in the sea, the more frantically they worked, striking as far as they could reach with their spears, and when a whale came close to the boat, they would give it a deep stab before pulling out the spear again. A few whales were so badly wounded that they quickly died, but most of them fought hard for life. They would be speared and would dive, surface, and be speared again, and between one boat and another, would get fearfully cut up. There were whales whose strength gradually ebbed away until they sank without a struggle. Other whales struggled forward, dragging their intestines behind them, their bodies waterlogged, swimming deep and snorting painfully, blood welling out of their numerous stab wounds. When a whale of this sort approached, the hunters would be filled with pity. 'Better finish this one off,' they would say, and they would gather around it to shorten its agony.

The people on the shore had now fallen silent, for though they rejoiced in the hunt, they were a little abashed at the slaughter, sobered to see the whales so mutilated and dying – those same whales that a little before had been swimming briskly and beautifully, with all the gleam and pride of the mighty ocean upon them. Yet other whales thrashed frantically among the boats, shooting half out of the water and charging forward regardless of obstacles, whipping up a foamy wake as they passed. These were the wild ones, a danger alike to boat and to man.

As the killing progressed, only a few of these whales continued to thrash about. Every time they approached a boat, they would be speared and thrust under the water. But suddenly, a whale reared right up by the gunwales of *The Troll*, and fell, dead, across her stern. All the crew leaped out and made their way to other boats. Kálvur, however, was too slow, and was dragged down with the boat.

This was too much for the people on the shore. The women buried their faces and wept, while the men, trying to take the incident with composure, could only stand speechless and stare.

Ketil, just at that moment, was sitting and scolding a young man who was trying to cut the spine of a stranded whale, but was cutting too low down, and meeting with little success. This irritated the old man. He was not worried about his son, who would find some way of freeing himself and coming up again after he had struck bottom. 'What a butter-fingers you are!' he said to the man who was cutting the spine. 'You carry a knife, and you can't even cut a whale. You're hacking at it like a booby.' Ketil had become so excited by the hunt, that he couldn't bear to see a stranded whale incompetently killed. He crawled down through the grass and out between the rocks on the shore. 'Get away from that whale, you bungler, and let me cut it,' he said. But the old man was over-eager, and not quite dextrous enough, for his knife slipped from his grasp, and fell against a rock. 'Oh, hell and damnation, now I'm ruining my knife,' he said.

'All the same, don't swear about it,' said a lay preacher who was standing nearby.

'Don't swear about it!' repeated Ketil, staring back at him. 'I ought to swear a good deal more than that. What else could any proper whale hunter do when he can hardly heave himself about? Sit still quietly, I suppose, while these butter-fingered boobies slash God's gifts in pieces? And now I've ruined my knife as well – the edge is bent right over.' But all the same, he finished off the whale.

The whale hunt was over. The last whale sank to the bottom. A solitary bubble rose slowly up from it and broke on the surface. The hunters wiped the sweat from their faces and put the wooden sheaths back on the blades of their spears. The rising tide was now bringing a flood of clear water into the bay, breaking over the dead whales and washing their gashes clean. The silt sank peacefully to the ocean floor again. The mist cleared, and the sun broke through and shone down on a calm sea, on the far blue hills of Vágar Island, and on green little Tindhólmur.

A flotilla of small boats was sailing into Seyrvágs Fjord, manned by triumphant hunters throwing their chests out and thinking themselves no end of fine fellows. They brought the news of their success to the village.

Next, there was a great buzz of activity in the District Sheriff's office, where the sheriff himself and two assessors were registering claims for compensation for damage to boats or to weapons. All three had the wrinkled brows and staccato speech of over-worked officialdom. In front of them stood a hunter holding out the wooden sheath of his whale spear, broken. 'Look,' he said, 'it's a completely new break – just look at it!' It was such a tight squeeze in the office, that anyone coming in could find room for himself only by squeezing the others tighter together. Then someone came in and tried to elbow the man with the spear-sheath out of the way, but only managed to make him snappish. Then the newcomer took the other man by the shoulders and said, 'I think you and your spear-sheath can wait for me. I've come from *The Troll*.' The man with the spear-sheath accepted this as no less than reasonable, and gave way to him.

Now someone came in with a torn pair of trousers. 'Just look here! A brand-new pair of trousers, and a spear tore them right down the thigh!' But the old assessor replied, 'Hell of a misfortune!' and went on to scold him. 'I don't think in all my born days I remember coming across a man so mean that after a hunt he wanted to put in a compensation claim for an old pair of bags.' And the man slipped away.

Kálvur did not apply to the assessors, although he had dislocated his shoulder and had been to the doctor's. He thought it was such a queer thing to do, to ask for money in this way. 'And you can never tell how you might be received, they might tell me it was all my own fault. After all, no one asked me to let a whale jump on me. Then people would make fun of me.'

Father and son were now wandering round among the houses, sniffing at doorways, searching for some place where they were cooking whale meat, for they knew that some boats had taken a potful home with them. Just then they were met by a couple of men who said that the District Sheriff had given them the job of fishing up such dead whales as had sunk in the bay. But they were short of help, and they asked if Ketil and Kálvur would care to join the party. 'Certainly, certainly, only too glad to,' said Ketil; 'but I hope you can hold on a minute, because we were just going in for a bite to eat. We left home in such a hurry there wasn't time to pack up anything to bring along.'

'You can eat at our place and welcome,' said the men. 'Come along with us.'

They were served porridge. 'This is a fine thing,' Ketil thought. 'We go wandering around, longing for a first taste of our kill, and we get porridge!' But they each had a good helping before going down to the boat.

It was dusk, and it had begun to drizzle. They got aboard a small boat and hoisted sail. There was a fair breeze, and they were soon away. 'Makes it all easy,' commented the men cheerfully. 'We weren't really anxious to row.' And they lounged forwards and began to chat. One man asked if the job of fishing up was paid in whale meat. Oh, yes, another told him; each man would get a hundredweight and a quarter – five stone of meat and five of blubber. 'Or it may be a straight hundredweight, I can't remember.'

Kálvur was so pleased that he had to speak. 'So that will be something like two hundredweight for the pair of us, Father.' And he chuckled at the thought.

The other men in the boat stared at him, but said nothing. Ketil steered the talk another way. 'How are you feeling now? Is that shoulder of yours giving you any trouble?'

Kálvur replied that he was all right now.

The others asked if he had been injured during the hunt. 'No, nothing to speak of,' said the old man. 'He went down with *The Troll*, and dislocated his shoulder, but the doctor pulled it into place again – and he did the job so easily, he wouldn't take a penny in payment.'

'Yes,' said one of the crew, 'he's certainly clever, though not everyone cares for him. Just before we came, I was talking with a man who had been up to the doctor's place to try and beg a drop or two of spirits, but got a flat refusal.'

'It was the man before him that would do you a favour and sell you some spirits – if he knew you. But it was dear, by God.'

'All the same, you need a doctor of that sort in a country like ours, where you can't buy a drop honestly when you want to.'

They reached the bay north of Tindhólmur, and began to search for the sunken whales. It was almost dark, and the tide was high. Several other boats were already there. They used long barbed poles for the work, for the water was no deeper than the length of an ordinary fishing rod, except in one or two places where it was twice as deep. They had three probes in the boat and the fourth man rowed. It was too dark to see the bottom, but they rowed gently and probed on all sides, feeling their way forward. At first they were all very keen on the job, and prodded away, while the old man was at the oars; but when an hour went by, and they had found nothing, the job began to bore them, and Kálvur dozed off in the bow.

'Now, my boy,' scolded Ketil, 'don't fall asleep when you're in a boat with strangers. You'll put us to shame!' And he slapped him on the back.

Kálvur woke with a start, thrust his probe down into the

water, and struck a whale. Then he came right to life. 'Hold on, hold on, Father – I've hit a whale!' he cried. Then he began to pull it slowly to the surface. The others got ready with the whale hook, leaning halfway over the gunwale. Then the great whale broke the surface. They could just pick out its long black form in the darkness. They banged the whale hook firmly into it with the help of a stone.

Then another boat loomed up out of the darkness, and there was a collision. A man came to the bow of the other boat to apologise. 'Sorry! We nearly ran you down.'

'It's all right, there's no harm done. You expect a bit of this on a whale hunt, and anyway, it's so dark, you can't see your own bow wave.' And the other boat disappeared into the night.

They towed the whale to the shore. They cut a hole in its jaw, fastened a stout line to it, and lashed it to a rock. Then they went back to look for more.

It was a pitch-black night, calm, and with a light drizzle. There was nothing you could take your bearings from except the dark outline of the hills on the northern side of the fjord against the sky, the lanterns that a few of the boats carried in their bows, and the faint white of the breakers on the skerries out to sea.

Ketil continued rowing with long, easy strokes. The damp darkness, the splash of the oars in the water, and the creak of the oarlocks made him doze off, and he dreamed he was rowing home with a full cargo of whale meat. A boat with a lantern in its prow, he took for his wife, who had come to ask how the hunt had gone.

'Everything went well, remarkably well.'

'You've got a heavily-laden boat there, my dear. Are you still loaded with stones?'

'Stones, no! That's meat, old girl, just meat.'

'Just as I thought,' replied his wife happily, 'a good whale hunter like you would never come home empty-handed, that I do know.'

The others in the boat leaned expectantly over the sides and stabbed down into the sea, noticing how often their probes became entangled in sea-weed, slid into holes, or hit rocks or sand on the seabed. Every time they saw something shining down in the water, they would call to Ketil to back water, in case it was a whale with its white intestines hanging out. The old man would halt the boat at once, but when they found it was only a jellyfish or a barnacle-covered rock, he would look up into the air, make a face, suck the drizzle out of his beard, and gently put the boat in motion again.

They recovered several more whales in the course of the night, and rowed to land with them, two or three in tow at a time. They became more nimble on each occasion, exchanged banter with the other boats, and took up more and more space on the line that was used for anchoring the salvaged whales. One time when they were landing a whale, Ketil went ashore, fumbled his way between the rocks, and was gone for some time. When he came back, he had his oilskin jacket rolled up under his arm.

'Well, well, we thought you'd gone for good,' said the men in the boat.

'I suppose it was a long time,' said Ketil. 'You can't ease yourself in the twinkling of an eye, when you're an old man.'

He put the oilskin down carefully under the bow thwart

and began rowing again. It was a whale's kidney he had been to get, for he proposed to take it to the doctor in recompense for his help to Kálvur.

When they returned to Seyrvágur, it was quite light.

'Ketil and Kálvur,' said the men, 'you must come home for a bite with us.'

They got porridge again. At this, they fumed and inwardly swore at the people of the house; but they ate a good meal. Then they went off to the other houses in search of some meat.

Later in the morning, the two walked down to the doctor's house, knocked at the door, and asked the maid if the doctor was at home.

'Yes, come in, he'll be along right away,' replied the maid. 'Come in here and sit down.'

They looked down at their muddy, home-made skin shoes, and hesitated, though they thought that they had such a good present with them that it didn't really matter even though they did leave a mark or two on the carpet. So they sat down just inside the door.

Soon the doctor came to them. 'Ah, good morning, good morning,' he said. He remembered them from before, when he had pulled Kálvur's shoulder into place. 'You've not come with another hunting injury, have you?' He sat down on a chair in front of them.

'No, nothing of that sort,' replied Ketil. 'It's just that we wanted to thank you for helping my son so much. It's just a little thing I've got here for you, which we hope you won't refuse.' He unwrapped the kidney from the oilskin jacket and offered it to the doctor, holding it up in his hands. 'It's absolutely fresh, just as it should be – I cut it out on Tindhólmur this morning.'

The doctor was staggered at the sight of this huge and bloody kidney, here in the middle of his smart living room. But he was polite, and said, 'Thank you, but this is too much, to bring me a whole kidney for myself.' He was so amazed, he could hardly utter a word, but simply stood there gaping.

His wife came in. She too was aghast and baffled. The doctor and his wife had both arrived in the country only recently, from Denmark, so that Faroese ways were strange to them. She had no idea that this thing was a whale's kidney. To her it was just something with blood oozing from it, that reminded her of recent and violent death. She did not doubt that Ketil was a human being, but he was not the usual kind she was accustomed to. And it cannot be denied that he did differ a little from the average Copenhagen businessman. He stood there in his home-made skin shoes, his loose breeches and long jacket. His blood-flecked beard hung down towards his belt, and on this hung a double sheath with a pair of white-handled knives, one above the other. And he was extending his earthy hands – holding up that bloody thing.

Ketil was puzzled at their reaction. 'Whatever's the matter with them?' he thought to himself. 'You needn't be afraid of it,' he assured them. 'This is a *fresh* whale's kidney I've brought you, a really fine, big, fresh kidney. You needn't be afraid of stomach troubles when you eat this one – I'll show you.' And he pulled out his vast, newly-whetted knife, sliced along the kidney, and said, 'Look how fresh it is – all the way through!'

The doctor's wife turned a little faint, and sat down on a chair. But the doctor took the kidney gratefully. 'We mustn't drive a man away, when he's come to present us with what he thinks is a great luxury,' he thought. 'Let's go into the kitchen,' he said, 'and we'll have a drop of coffee.'

Ketil and Kálvur were given something to eat and drink; and when they left, the doctor gave them a flask of brandy. 'This isn't such a bad pick-me-up when you get home from a hunt,' he remarked.

'A real blessing to us, that doctor,' they agreed as they left. A little later, they slipped behind a hillock, and each had a good mouthful from the flask. 'We'd better save the rest till this evening,' said the old man. So they put the flask away, and took a boat over to Tindhólmur, because now the whale tickets were to be issued by the District Sheriff, authorising each householder to take away his share of the kill.

The Seyrvágur men have a single house on Tindhólmur, which they use when they go to the islet for the fowling, or to round up their sheep. It has just one living room with a kitchen range and some big cupboard bunks. Up in the roof hangs a fowling rope, and slung across the beams is gear of various kinds. In one corner is a small table with six white mugs and a coffee pot. The house smells of mountain and earth, of decaying wood, and turf.

Around the little table by a window of this house, dressed in an assortment of oilskins, sat the District Sheriff and his assistants, reckoning up the shares of whale meat which every family was entitled to. Each of them had a mug of coffee in one hand and a pencil in the other, and they sat there laughing and joking. They looked just like the hunters, but they kept themselves a little apart from them, since they were better dressed, and had clean hands.

Two schoolmasters sat on a bench by the stove. They had been through a swamp and got themselves really muddy, so that they would look like real whale-hunters. They supped coffee and made eyes at the womenfolk who were standing nearby. They stirred in their sugar with a sheep's rib, which they passed from one to the other. The womenfolk crowded around them, and stood looking at them from the windows and the doors, because they were both bachelors.

The rest of the house was packed with wet hunters waiting for their whale tickets. They sat around, silent, while the rain lashed the roof, and the peat fire glowed behind the bars of the stove.

After the whale tickets had been issued, Ketil and Kálvur joined up with a boat that was searching for whales that had been overlooked. They found a large whale that had come ashore in a little bay some distance away, and lay covered in seaweed. They were delighted, for such whales belong to the finders. Kálvur simply laughed, and made faces at a man standing up in another boat and eying them enviously. But Ketil and Kálvur were not alone – there were five in the boat.

When they got on shore again, the District Sheriff was on his way to auction off the whales which were to defray the compensation claims. They could pick him out by his official hat. He stood on a rock in the middle of a crowd of people, offering each whale in turn. Bids came up from the crowd. The District Sheriff would repeat each bid, until everyone was silent. Then he would rap with his pencil on the neck of the man just in front of him, who was recording buyers and prices.

Ketil and Kálvur now went up to a stretch of grass to sit

down. The weather was fine and dry. 'Father,' said Kálvur, 'we've done pretty well this time, haven't we?'

'Yes, that's true enough,' said the old man. 'We got a good share of that whale we found, and we also have our payment for fishing up the sunk whales.'

'Yes, and we saved our fare to Seyrvágur,' added Kálvur. 'I got my shoulder put right for nothing, and that flask we got from the doctor ought to be counted in as well.'

Ketil laughed. 'Yes, yes, there's something in what you say. But we ought not to sit here. If the prices aren't too high, we ought to buy ourselves a hundredweight or two more. It'll be long enough before I go whale hunting again, I think.' So they went along.

But now as they were going down to the auction, they met Lias Berint, a little old man in a tattered coat and worn-out skin shoes. 'Hello there, Ketil,' he said. 'I knew you'd still have enough left in you so you wouldn't be sitting idle at home when there was a whale hunt in the island.'

'Oh, yes, I've come along all right, but it's more from habit, let me tell you, than for any strength I've got left for the job.'

Lias Berint whispered in his ear, 'Just listen to me a minute.'

'Kálvur, wait here till I come back,' said Ketil.

They disappeared from view. Lias Berint gave him some spirits. When they returned, they had their arms round each other's shoulders, and they were beginning to laugh and sing. 'Yes, yes, age is beginning to tell on both of us now, but in the old days – then we showed them a thing or two, eh?' And they strutted and danced around. 'Now we must go and do some bidding,' said Ketil. 'We aren't so worn out that we can't buy a whale or two.' They pushed forward to where the District Sheriff was conducting the auction.

'Number 183 – six hundredweight,' called out the District Sheriff. 'Any bid for that?'

Three kroner a hundredweight – three and a half – several bids of four kroner. Then a jump to six kroner. It was finally knocked down for nine kroner.

'Number 184 – thirty-six hundredweight. Any bid for that?'

The bidding paused at four and a half kroner. Ketil bid five and a half, and was overbid at six and a half. 'I'm going to get this whale,' he resolved. He made a further bid of seven and a half kroner. This got him the whale. The District Sheriff turned around to see who it was, wrote down the name and gave Ketil his ticket. The old man now pushed his way out of the crowd, proud of himself, and holding his head high. But when he came up to the stretch of grass where his son was, he blanched to see how staggered Kálvur was. 'Father,' said Kálvur, 'a thirty-six hundredweight whale at seven and a half kroner a hundredweight – doesn't it come to a frightful lot of money all told?'

'Yes, yes, it does ... .' The old man's head fell to his chest. He lacked the strength to reckon up just how much it was. Kálvur began to weep, and held his hands in front of his face so that folk would not see. Ketil was completely sobered up by the enormity of what he had done. 'Lord preserve us, I could lie down and die,' he sighed. 'Never in all our born days have we ever run ourselves into such a big debt. But what's done is done, and we must just face our fate. I can't go back and cancel it – that would bring down shame on me.' They did indeed look a pair of tragic figures when they went down to look for their whale.

In the afternoon the weather took a turn for the worse. The open boats could not start for home, so they went back to Seyrvágur again. Most of the crews took their whales along with them whole, to cut up in the village. When Ketil and Kálvur reached the mainland with their whale, it was so late that they could not do anything with it that evening. The only thing they could do was to get people to help them drag it well up on the beach and leave it there.

Now you could get boiled whale meat in any house you called at, which was some consolation to them. 'If only they'd given us meat instead of that blessed porridge,' Ketil told his son, 'that drop of spirits I drank wouldn't have done anything to me, and then the whale would never have been bought.' They fed well, and then went back up to the hillock to look for their brandy flask, but it was with heavy hearts that they took out the cork and drank a drop or two. They just sat with their heads hung low.

But when they had supped a third mouthful, Kálvur raised his head and said, 'Father, it's not such an enormous amount, even if we have got two and a half tons of whale meat. Nobody can tell when there'll be another whale killing. There might even be a war.'

'No, it's good to have the meat,' answered Ketil, 'but it's the bill, my lad, when *that* comes. Your mother will be at her wits' end when she learns how we've run ourselves into such a big debt.' They had a fourth sup at the brandy. 'But it's silly, perhaps, to get downhearted over this business. We haven't stolen the meat; and we haven't brought shame on ourselves.

And if worse comes to worst, we can always sell some of the meat when everyone else has eaten up theirs.' They cheered up again; the darkness lifted a bit from them and they once again took heart. So they put the flask away again and decided to go to the dance and get themselves warmed up; but when they came to the dance-hall, Kálvur slipped away again.

He did not dare to join in, lest people should remark on his odd way of dancing. So he went back to the brandy flask and drank himself full. When he came back to the dance, he was no longer bashful. He went right up to the ring dance and bade folk make way for him, for here was the man who had bought a 36-hundredweight whale, and had gone to the bottom of the sea in *The Troll*. The girls shrieked at him, because he would take hold of them round the waist, and tell them he'd like to go courting with them.

People laughed at him and said, 'Step up and give us a song, Kálvur.'

'No, I'm no singer,' replied Kálvur. I only know "The Boasting Ballad", and every man can boast of that – but not many can say they've been to the bottom of the sea with *The Troll*!' And then he mimicked the way the whale shot up half way out of the water and clumped down dead, on top of the boat.

Then Ketil came and told him to join quietly in the ring dance near him, and not go round making a spectacle of himself. 'Don't you see that folk are laughing at you?' said the old man. Kálvur fell silent, because he realised that perhaps he had indeed done something odd.

The house was full of hunters who had come to dance themselves dry. Steam rose from them, and drops of water lay on their jackets and oilskins. The air was cloudy with dust, and it lay heavy on the chest, so men were hacking and coughing, crowding together and getting red in the face, but also laughing and wagging their heads about with happiness, for they were celebrating a successful hunt.

It got late. Now Ketil and Kálvur, tired of dancing, thought it best to go in search of somewhere to get a little sleep. Of course, you sleep anywhere after a whale-hunting party. They entered a barn. But a boat's crew had already burrowed into the hay, and as they went in, they trod on one head after another, and fists sprang up out of the hay and thrashed blindly about in the dark. Ketil and Kálvur beat as fast a retreat as they could. They did not even go down by the ladder, but jumped straight down into the lane. Then they heard a real babel of voices. 'Who the hell do you think you're hitting?' 'What the devil do you think I'm going to do, if you stamp on my eyeballs with a pair of bloody sea boots?'

Ketil and Kálvur looked into several houses, but every one was full. Men were lying on benches and on the floor and snoring around the roaring stoves. In one house they entered, Lias Berint was sitting by the fire. He had undressed from his belt downwards, and had hung his trousers up to dry. He was temporarily dressed in a shirt he had found somewhere.

'There's room for you here,' Lias Berint laughed at them, 'if you don't mind sitting straight up and down.'

Ketil and Kálvur thought there would be little rest in that. So they went into a field and pulled a small haystack over themselves.

The next day, great heaps of meat were stacked in front of every door in Seyrvágur. Happy men, their faces aglow with what they had already eaten, were singing the old Faroese ballads as they carried on the work of salting the meat and hanging it up. Smoke rose from every house, from the fires under the huge cooking-pots; and even the old bedridden folk managed to totter as far as the house eaves, as they always do when a big catch is brought into the village.

Little gangs of well-fed children were running wild across the fields in a way that would never be allowed in ordinary times.

Yes, a whale-killing is a blessing for everyone!

CHAPTER TWO

There were only two rooms in Ketil's house, the bedroom and the kitchen. Along the wall that faced the mountainside were four cupboard bunks, two in each room. The old folk slept in one of the bedroom bunks, and Kálvur had the other, while the kitchen bunks were now used as storage space. But in former times, these too had been used for sleeping. Ketil and his wife had had eleven children, and they had to be put somewhere. But now there was plenty of room, for all of them had got married and gone, except Kálvur, the youngest.

The morning after they had fetched home the whale meat, father and son were lying in their bunks chewing tobacco. It was well on in the morning, but they were lying in and recuperating after their labours. A kitten was sitting on the floor and playing with Ketil's beard, which hung over the edge of his bunk. Kálvur was lying down, with the flask which they had got from the doctor in his hand. He was admiring the label, which he thought was very beautiful. On the floor near them stood a spittoon. Every now and then they craned their necks and spat into it.

'Father, has there ever been so much whale meat in the house before?' asked Kálvur.

'No, never anywhere near as much. There's so much that all your brothers and sisters could take away a share. The menfolk are all at sea now, so they didn't get any, but you know what? I wouldn't get a penny from them in return. And what's worse, they're like a cow stuck in a swamp – give her a hand, and she'll never do anything for herself again. So I wouldn't dare to give them any. And your mother would bite my head off if I let her daughters-in-law carry off any of our whale meat.'

There was a great racket outside the house – grandchildren. Now there was meat in the house, you couldn't open the door without their pushing in to beg some. They were insatiable.

Kálvur put his hand to his stomach. 'Father, I think I could do with something to eat.'

'Ah well, I'll go next door and get us a bite of cold meat. Your mother has gone off to fetch home some peats. When she comes back, she'll give us some hot.'

Ketil went into the kitchen, where the pot was standing on a peat creel with what was left over from the last cooking. But when he got there, not a scrap of meat was to be seen. But there was a sort of rumbling on the roof, and when he looked out of the window, he saw thirteen grandchildren down in the fields, sprawling around and squabbling over the big piece of meat they had fished up through the old-fashioned smoke hole in the roof of Ketil's house.

Ketil and Kálvur were annoyed at this, and went into the kitchen to drink milk instead. But it was not the same as eating a nice piece of whale meat. When Ketil's wife came back, she scolded them for finishing off all the meat that had been left over. 'You'll make yourselves ill with it,' she said.

'I only wish it had been us,' snorted Kálvur.

When the old woman heard that it was the children who had taken the meat, she seized her big dyeing pole and chased them all right away from the house. 'Just let me catch you back here again, you little wretches!' she shouted. But when she came in again, she began to feel sorry for them. 'Bless them, what else could they do but hover round the catch? Their fathers are all away at the fishing, and they didn't get a share at all.' And she cooked an extra helping for their lunch.

The following days were devoted to haymaking, but it went forward slowly, because it was poor drying weather, and they had no real heart for the work. That bill that would be coming for the whale meat – they could not get it out of their minds. The old woman was the worst. She constantly cast it in the teeth of her menfolk that they had landed the household in a real mess, because they could not pay the bill for the meat, and they would run into debt. This was the biggest disgrace that could come on them – not to be able to pay their way. And she wept and wept.

Ketil agreed with her that they were in a fix. 'But take it easy, lassie,' he said. 'We've weathered so many storms together before now – never let it be said we won't weather this one too.' And he pushed out his lips from behind his beard and gave his wife a kiss. Kálvur blushed at this, for they were out in the open field, where the whole village could see them.

But the old woman would not be comforted. She said she could see no way out of their trouble. 'We've never owed a penny in all our born days,' she said, 'and now in our old age, we've run into a debt we can't pay, that we need 270 kroner to clear.'

Ketil became weary of this. He stuffed his mouth full of tobacco, and told her to end her grumbling. 'It's no good going on like this. What with the south-west showers and your weeping, how shall we ever get this hay dry?'

In the evening, the old woman tied a scarf on her head, took her stick in her hand, and like all the other village women, went out to do the milking.

The first milking-woman who greeted her remarked, 'You got a good load of meat from the hunt.'

'Yes, God be praised, we did pretty well from it.' Then she said no more, but carried on her way.

The next woman said, 'You didn't get a bad share of the whale meat, did you?'

'Well, that's what you expect when there are some skilful fellows on the job,' replied Ketil's wife.

The third woman said, 'You got a fine lot from the Seyrvágur hunt, didn't you?'

'I wish Old Nick would shove a gag in some of your mouths! And I wouldn't mind if you were flat out on the floor and the whale across your guts!' Then Ketil's wife disappeared among the cows. The third milking-woman looked after her in astonishment.

They agreed to send Kálvur to Seyrvágur to ask the District Sheriff when the bills for the whale meat would come. It was always interesting to find that out.

Kálvur tried to get out of the job, because he found it

embarrassing to go among strangers to ask them things, but he soon gave in. He was in a good humour when he set out, feeling himself no end of a grand fellow, having so important an errand to Seyrvágur, to the District Sheriff himself. 'If people ask me where I'm going,' he thought, 'I can tell them I'm going – to the District Sheriff! "That's some errand you've got, Kálvur," they will say.' And he thrust his chest out, swung his arms, and strode on his way.

He thought it was great fun to be out on his own, to be able to do what he liked, even to belch, to ease himself, or such like. He wished that some young woman would come along and want him. It would be fun to have been able some time to have hugged a girl really close, but it was so embarrassing to make the first move oneself. 'If only one would come after me!' he thought. When he reached the wall that enclosed the Seyrvágur infield, he took off his homemade skin shoes and pushed them between the stones, put on his black leather shoes in their place, and carried on down into the village.

Down by the shore he saw a crowd of men standing by a boathouse. They were seamen who had just come ashore from their ship. These men did not talk to one another, but just stood there, staring in unison across the fjord, with their hands thrust deep into their trouser pockets, and their heads sunk down on their chests. Kálvur went up to them and greeted them. 'Can you tell me where the District Sheriff lives?' he asked them. They did not reply for a time, but then one of them lifted a foot and pointed out the house with his shoe. Kálvur shuddered a little. He thought this was too grand a house for him to venture into. But he plucked up his courage, and went over.

When he entered the house, the District Sheriff was sitting

there in his shirt sleeves, dealing with some documents for an English ship that was in the harbour.

'Is the District Sheriff here?' asked Kálvur, with a trembling voice.

'That's me,' said the man in his shirt sleeves.

'You, sir?' asked Kálvur dubiously.

'Me, yes, me, God help me,' lamented the District Sheriff, springing up out of his chair and standing on his toes to make himself look a great tall fellow.

Kálvur turned pale. 'I'm sorry, I thought the District Sheriff looked different. I wanted to ask when the whale-meat bills will be coming out.'

'The whale-meat bills – yes, when the devil will I be through with those whale-meat bills?' The District Sheriff paused, and fell deep in thought, and tapped his head in several places to try to get something moving inside. He stuck his thumbs into his shirt sleeves, and looked straight up at the ceiling. Kálvur stood in the doorway, full of admiration at his fine manner. But he also reflected that it would never do to look straight up in the air in this way in their old-fashioned house, because the hens sat on the crossbeams, and at any time you might get an eyeful.

'Yes,' said the District Sheriff at last, coming right over to Kálvur. 'I can tell you. The whale-meat bills will not be issued before the New Year – definitely not before the New Year.' Then he turned on his heel and went back to his work on the English ship's papers.

Kálvur left the house. He felt pleased with himself as he came away, and chuckled as he walked. 'If it's no worse than that to go into a fine big house, I shan't be afraid another time.'

He stepped along jauntily, flapping his coat-tails and crowing with satisfaction, but quietly, lest anyone should hear. This was a manner that was very apt to come over Kálvur when he was pleased with himself.

Before he left the village, he went into a shop and bought himself half a pound of biscuits. It would have been a great shame to have been in Seyrvágur and not to have got something good – and sweetstuff was no load to carry.

When Kálvur returned from Seyrvágur, Klávus was there on a visit. Ketil and his wife snorted with vexation at this wretched snooping fellow who had dropped in and made himself at home, so that they couldn't exchange as much as a word with Kálvur.

Klávus sprawled along the bench and lit his pipe. 'Been over to Seyrvágur, Kálvur?' he asked. 'Some important errand, I suppose.'

Ketil and his wife stood by the fire, winking and grimacing at Kálvur, to warn him to say nothing. Kálvur sat there with a bowl on his knees, eating his supper. He felt like showing off a bit, so he said, 'Yes, I was in Seyrvágur – on an errand to the District Sheriff.' Then he swallowed a big spoonful and looked straight at Klávus.

Klávus now lost all urge to stay. 'No, it's silly, hanging about here. You ought to turn me out. One really shouldn't waste time like this.' And off he went.

For a long time now, Klávus had been devoutly religious; but everyone has his besetting weakness to struggle with. Klávus's was the illegal removal of driftwood from the foreshore, and that was why he did not like to hear the District Sheriff named.

But Klávus was conscious of his failing and struggled against it. As long as the wind was blowing from the land, he could keep a grip on himself, and felt no urge to go stealing driftwood. But if the wind kept blowing off shore for a very long time, he might happen to 'find' a pole in one of the sheds in which the villagers dried their fish and mutton. And if a lamb's carcass happened to be hanging from the pole, he might possibly take that along as well. But when the onshore wind returned, he could no longer hold out – he had to succumb to temptation. But everything is wisely ordained in this world, and it was precisely through this theft of driftwood that Salvation came to Klávus. One day, just as he was slipping a plank into his shed, a Seventh Day Adventist preacher came up to him unexpectedly.

'You who are stealing driftwood, begetting children, marrying and giving in marriage! The Kingdom of Heaven is at hand! The seventh seal is opened, and the day is nigh when the Beast shall rise up out of the sea with the name of blasphemy in its mouth. You who are seeking for wood along the shore, take upon you the white robes of the Lamb and bow your knee before the Throne!'

Klávus was converted then and there. He pushed the plank away from him, and the two of them gave themselves up to prayer. Since that time he had always prayed, every time he pushed stolen driftwood into his shed. Once, he had even wept bitterly as he was carrying home his flotsam, so deeply did he repent of his condition. That time it was a spirit barrel he had found, and punishment followed close on his sin. He fell asleep dead drunk by his shed wall, and a grazing horse came and bit the beard from the side of his chin that faced upwards, leaving his red beard as usual on the other side. But Klávus accepted his punishment with resignation.

When Klávus had gone, Ketil's wife lit the peat fire. When the smoky stage was over, all three of them sat around the blaze. A tiny oil lamp flickered on the window sill. Up on the beams sat the gently cackling hens. You could hear the cow, the other side of the partition, licking the planking in front of her. The kitten was running about way under the benches. He had discovered a mouse that was busy somewhere at the back of the timberwork. The old woman was knitting, and you could hear the click of her needles. The conversation was in few words, and those whispered.

'There's certainly plenty of time before the bill has to be paid,' said Ketil. 'And perhaps the Lord will provide us with the means.'

'It's a bit better,' answered his wife. 'I'll try and save wherever I can – on tea, for instance; we can drink milk-and-water instead. And I shall buy no more coffee – we shall use burnt corn.' She got up and put out the lamp. 'The fire is burning up so well, there's no need to keep this light going.'

Now seven grandchildren came bursting in, every one of them with a bag of sweets in his hand. 'Look here! Would you like a toffee?'

'That is kind of you. Who's given you these?'

'Father was paid off today.'

The old woman looked at Ketil. 'Perhaps he could help you a bit. He could have meat in return, or we could let him have the money back later.'

'Yes, I think I'll go over and see him.'

The old man did not really like going into the houses of his

40

daughters-in-law. They were so houseproud, he thought – could not bear to see skin shoes or tobacco-spit. You hardly dared to cross a doorstep, everything was so scoured and scrubbed.

He went into the kitchen and squatted down on a low chair right by the door, and looked about him. Here there was brassware and linoleum, curtains, crocheted and embroidered drapery – everything you could think of, and every scrap of wood was painted. Still, he thought, if they can afford it, and like to have things this way, who are we to criticise?

'Is the lad in?' the old man asked as his daughter-in-law appeared.

'He's in the dining-room. Carry on in, Father.'

The old man hesitated a little before he went, because he knew his daughter-in-law did not really care for him, but he plucked up courage. 'Maybe I do smell of the peat fire and the cow byre,' he thought, 'but I pay my own way, and nobody can drive me out of house and home.' So he stuffed his hat into his jacket pocket and went in.

'Fine weather we're having,' Ketil began.

His son looked up. 'Yes, good weather,' he replied absently. 'Extraordinarily good weather.' He sat at the table, fingering through a great heap of papers.

'That's a proper heap of letters you've had.'

'Letters? No, these are bills.' He looked up at his father. 'It costs a lot of money to keep going these days.'

'You're right there, it certainly costs money. Has your ship paid you off today?'

'Yes, that's it here – all these bills.'

The old man stared at the heap of papers. 'Can you live on these?'

'No, but now nobody can turn us out of the house for the next six months, and I've paid for what we ate this summer.'

'But life becomes one long worry,' said Ketil critically. 'We old folk know better than that.'

'You know better? Well, if we wanted to bury ourselves under a heap of earth and live on fish skins and watery soup, we might pile up a bit of money. But what property have you got?'

'I've got my house.'

The son looked up at his father. 'Yes, but what sort of house? Turf and fleas.'

The old man did not know what to say in return, but he knew that there were seven children in his son's house, and that winter was on the way.

'You've got a lot of whale meat,' said the son. 'Can we have a bit from you?'

'Certainly you can, but it's another matter whether we can pay the bill when it comes. I'm seventy now, an old man.'

'Pay the whale-meat bill!' laughed the son. 'Who would have believed that *you* would have run up a mortgage to buy whale meat?'

The old man's eyes blazed, and he threw out his chest. 'God preserve me from the disgrace of ending my days in beggary!' Then he went. When he was outside, he brushed away a tear from his cheek. 'Young people these days have such strange ways. I just don't know where I stand.'

Ketil's wife pulled a very long face when she heard how things were. 'She ought to be properly ashamed of herself,' she said of her daughter-in-law. 'If I had my way, she wouldn't be going around in her powder and paint all day. But those poor children!'

Kálvur sat quietly on the bench, listening. He thought this was all very bad. Mankind was so evil that he trembled. God could hardly be bothered any longer. It looked as though He had washed His hands of the world, and was now letting the Devil do just what he liked. 'Let those lost sheep find their own way if they can, and much good may it do them.' But he said a prayer for himself.

The next day, Ketil again went across to his son, to suggest that they should go fishing. 'What use will that be?' answered his son. 'We'd only have yet another bill to pay.'

The old man could not understand this. 'Even if we caught nothing, it wouldn't do us any harm – it won't cost anything.'

'We'll have to pay for the petrol.'

'No, I wasn't thinking of taking a motorboat. We've still got our old rowboat lying there. We can put that into good enough shape to take us.'

'Oh, no,' answered his son. 'You don't get me rowing a cockleshell like that all the way out to the fishing bank.'

'Well, well, then, there's nothing more to be said,' sighed the old man. He went and asked his other sons and sons-in-law, but they all said the same. 'What, sweat away with oars all that way again? Not likely.'

So Ketil and Kálvur had to try by themselves. They got the boat turned over on trestles, but then a spell of bad weather came, and they had to postpone the job.

CHAPTER THREE

Ketil sat by the peat fire and listened to the noise of the breakers echoing in the hillside. 'There ought to be an oar timber among the stuff thrown up in West Bay tonight,' he said.

'Are you short of oars?' asked his wife.

'I certainly am – I can't take our boat out till I get one. And I'd have to pay the store a good sum if I bought it there.'

'Well then,' said his wife, 'go over to West Bay, and you'll find timber for your oar right enough.'

'I'd certainly like to,' Ketil replied, 'but how can I? I don't own any share in the foreshore rights.'

'Don't be such a fool. Who bothers about things like that any more? Does Klávus?'

'Klávus, that old thief! Do you think I'm going to walk in unlawful paths just because he does?'

'Go over to the pastor, then, and ask him for leave to search for driftwood.'

Ketil's spirits rose. He decided to go over to the pastor right away. He sprang up and asked his wife to pass him his skin shoes.

'You'd better tidy yourself up before you go,' his wife warned him.

But he thought this quite unnecessary; he just pulled a few strands of chewing tobacco off his beard. There were three dead spiders clinging to the front of his sweater, and he brushed these away too. Then off he went.

When he reached the rectory, the pastor was sitting there in his shirt sleeves, reading the Book of Job. He asked Ketil what he could do for him.

'I wanted to ask your permission to search for driftwood. I happen to be in great need of a piece of timber for an oar.'

'Search and welcome,' replied the pastor, 'and the peace of God go with you.'

So Ketil went away, full of good will towards the pastor. 'I'll grant him one thing – he's not so stuck up he won't talk with humble folk,' he thought. But he reflected that the pastor's words about the peace of God would certainly be of little avail, for Klávus was a real brute, and would be bound to show his teeth if the two of them should meet on the beach. Nowadays, nobody else here in the village except Klávus was in the habit of searching for driftwood, so he might well take the view that anyone else coming to West Bay was poaching on his preserves. But Ketil didn't intend to be elbowed out. He had now received permission to search the beach. Klávus certainly had not.

The weather got worse and worse. It was pitch dark, the heavens were black, and the air howling with squalls. Flashes of pale green lightning momentarily lit up the line of the hills and the foaming waterfalls, while the thunder crashed among the mountains.

Later, Ketil and Kálvur opened the door of their house. A sudden squall ripped it from their hands. 'Poof, the north-easter is pretty rough this morning,' said Ketil. And they battled their way into it.

They had to walk with care, for the wind was treacherous. At times it would be dead calm; then a rumbling would be heard from far off, like the rolling of a mighty wheel, and a whirlwind would be upon them, ripping the grass from the hillside, blasting the water out of the streams, and lashing the village unmercifully with spray from the sea, while the houses creaked and shook to their foundations.

Ketil and Kálvur went forth on their search for driftwood. They took a line with them, and a gun, and each had a spiked staff in his hand. 'Ugh, how dark it is,' said Kálvur. 'I'm scared of it.'

'Don't be so foolish. At your age you shouldn't be afraid. It only draws the evil down upon you. Pray that Jesus may be with us, and that through His help we will find an oar timber.'

Kálvur agreed to do this.

It was hard finding the way. Ketil went first. He walked with bent knees, but taking long strides, and feeling his way with his staff. Now and then he stumbled in peat holes or dips, but he never fell far, for he was bent forward so much, and he was soon on his feet again. But he grumbled constantly.

'Now, up we get again, and the Lord watch over me! This business will be the death of me,' he would mutter, every time he fell down.

The young man fared rather better, for he heard the thumps when the old man fell, and looked out for himself. He was very much afraid. He thought that the Devil was out there in the darkness, and he felt that something was following close behind him, something with talons that wanted to seize hold of him. It was worst when the foaming torrents slashed through the darkness ahead of him, as the lightning flashed and the thunder rolled among the mountains. Then he would shiver right down his spine, and he would be on the point of crying out for help, but he would check himself, and pray inwardly, 'Be with us, Jesus, and help us to find an oar timber!'

But as they went on their way, the darkness faded and a new day was born – a morning hungry for light, full of windswept clouds and frothing streams. Kálvur regained his courage. 'There, now, we didn't die after all,' he thought. He gaped up at the darker part of the sky, to the westward. Now he only prayed, 'Jesus, help us to find an oar timber.'

They reached a sheep shelter and sat down to recover their strength. Now was a good time to have a bite to eat. They had with them an ember-baked loaf and a piece of dried mutton. Ketil said, 'Kálvur, it's better if you have the mutton, you poor lad. Young folk need good food. All I need is a bit of the bread.'

But Kálvur would not agree. 'It's better if you have the mutton,' he answered, 'because I'm stronger than you are.'

Then Ketil had to laugh. 'Yes, I think you are the stronger of us – you've grown up before we noticed it. How old are you now?'

'Twenty-four.'

'About right for getting married, then.'

Kálvur blushed and turned aside his face. Of course, now and then he had done a bit of courting with Klávus's daughter, but as for getting married, he would never be able to bring himself to the point of doing that.

They had to carry on, to prevent themselves freezing, wet through as they were. 'Oh, the Lord help me,' groaned Ketil, 'I'm as stiff as a board every time I get up. If only there's an oar timber down there, when we get to the beach!'

They reached the point where they could look down into the bay. Their good humour returned, and they made themselves merry about Klávus. 'He'll just be setting out from his house,' they said. 'Whatever will he say when he sees us here?'

A haze of spray was hanging over the bay. The foam-crested breakers rolled in from the sea, smashing up between the rocks and boulders, and flooding over the beach and the foot of the cliff right up to the grass; and then, their power spent, they ran back in gentle, muddy streams. The spray shot high up the narrow clefts and gaps in the foot of the cliffs, while the storm whipped the top parts away in great flecks, and blew them far in over the moorland.

When they got down from the hillside, they lowered their voices, and broke into a trot. Their faces became serious, and they clenched their fists inside their mittens. They pressed on towards the shore, almost feeling their way forwards as they struggled down the slope. Their eyes protruded with eagerness for their quarry, but they trembled a little at the knees lest the inscrutable sea should have cast up something frightful onto the beach.

Kálvur wiped cold sweat from his forehead. 'Father,' he said, 'if we found a dead body down here, what should we do?'

'Let us pray God that it will not happen; but if it should, then we must carry it home and report the matter.'

'Would you dare to move a dead body, Father? It might haunt you.'

'You can't always avoid doing what you wouldn't dare to do,' replied the old man. 'But it would be worse to walk away and leave it lying helpless on the shore.'

'Would it haunt worse then, Father?'

'Of course, what would you expect, if it was left lying here, and was never laid to rest in the churchyard?'

Kálvur trembled until his teeth chattered, and he wondered about human life. If it had occurred to him that they might possibly find a dead body, he would never have come along. To be haunted by ghosts, whether you took the body home or left it lying there, was dreadful. He felt already as though something were rustling along behind him.

They went down to the water's edge. There was no corpse there, and Kálvur took courage again. He found a lump of pumice, which the Faroe Islanders believe will protect a house from being struck by lightning. 'Father,' he said, 'shall I take this home?'

'Certainly,' replied the old man, 'but there should be a piece there already. Your grandfather put one into the foundation, when he built the house.'

Kálvur thought he would take it along all the same. He had often thought that in a thunderstorm, it would be good to have one under his pillow.

They found a few codfish and some scraps of driftwood. 'We might as well gather them up,' said Ketil, 'they can all be used.' So they carried everything to a little hollow on the eastern side of the bay. Then they walked westward, right round the bay, but without finding any real piece of timber. 'A piece can still turn up,' they said, consoling themselves. 'The day is long enough.' And their journey had not been altogether fruitless. Fish, and fragments of wood were all around the place, and now and then they shot a bird or two.

Later, when they came eastward again, they saw a man standing by their hollow. It was Klávus, who was filling his creel with their fish. They were astonished at this, and stopped. But when Klávus saw them, he chuckled at them in a friendly manner. 'Oh, it's you two who have come here, is it? I was just thinking that your fish were lying so near the sea that the breakers might easily wash them away again. If you'll help me up with this creel, I'll carry them a bit higher up.'

Ketil laughed inwardly. 'The way this fellow wriggles out of difficulties,' he thought. He said, 'It won't do any harm to leave the fish lying here, I shouldn't think.' And he took the creel and emptied the fish back into the hollow.

'Maybe not, maybe not,' chuckled Klávus. 'In any case there are now three of us to look after them. I had a few fish as well, that I threw into this heap, so perhaps it would be best if I put them back into the creel.' He stooped down again towards the heap of fish.

'No, you'd better leave them alone, Klávus,' said Ketil. 'I think that what's here, we'll count as ours.'

'Yes, of course – Oh, no, I wasn't thinking of taking anything away – I just thought I'd, er – Anyway, have you had any luck out here today? Has any decent bit of wood been thrown ashore?'

'No, we've found nothing but scraps.'

'Yes, yes – it's just as usual then. You don't often get anything much, except a few bits to put on the fire. If Jesus will only watch over us, so that we reach home in safety, that's all we can hope for on this trip, my friends. It cannot be so many more days, I'm sure of it, before we reach the last time, when there will be signs in the sun and in the moon. See how the windows of heaven are filled, and ready to discharge their waters upon this vale of misery. Behold: the rivers shall overflow their banks, and the sea shall swallow up the whole world.' Then Klávus left them.

Ketil roared with laughter. 'That's put him in a bad mood all right! He didn't like having to give up his plunder.'

But Kálvur was astonished. It was the first time he had seen anybody steal anything, and he was disappointed when he saw no misfortune come upon Klávus as a consequence. His face did not become black, neither did the Devil come and run off with him.

The next time they saw Klávus, he was carrying a great plank over his shoulder.

'That fellow has the Devil's own luck,' grumbled Ketil and Kálvur. 'That was just the plank we were looking for.'

'But where did he get the plank from?' they asked each other. 'We've walked around the bay from end to end, and it couldn't have been floating in the water, because we'd have spotted it quite as quickly as Klávus.' They agreed that it must be that Klávus knew how to search better than they did. 'But wait a minute,' said Ketil, 'and we'll find out what tricks he uses.' And they hid themselves among the stones.

They saw Klávus walked down to the shore line again. He walked slowly forward, climbed onto a great boulder, and looked out over the sea; then he got down again, and poked with his stick into the seaweed and scraps of rubbish thrown up by the tide. 'Well, we can do that ourselves,' thought Ketil and Kálvur. But now Klávus came to a great bank of foam, and poked his stick into that. They were astounded when they saw him actually walk into the foam, feeling his way forward with his stick, and disappear. A little later he came out again with a piece of wood and a catfish. Then Ketil and Kálvur realised where the plank had come from, and hurried down. 'The fellow's cute and clever all right, but just wait till another day.' And they set about digging into the foam banks.

The weather improved, though the wind remained the same. The day gradually wore on. Kálvur was beginning to get bored, and wanted to get back home. 'We've walked about ever such a long time, and had nothing but bread to eat,' he said. 'I want some whale meat and a dry change of clothes.'

'You shouldn't be the first of us two to give up,' said Ketil sharply. 'I wasn't afraid of being wet through when I was your age. I think we ought to stay here as long as we can see. The weather's clearing up, and it won't be so dark as to make it difficult for us to find our way home, even after sunset.'

'Yes, but I shall want something to eat.'

'We've got bread.'

But no, Kálvur did not want bread. 'I want a proper meal.'

'What proper meal do you suppose we can get in this wilderness? Go down to the water and see if you can find any mussels, and I'll see whether I can get a fire going.'

So they baked mussels and ate their fill of them.

Later, in the evening, Ketil and Kálvur heard a cry for help. Kálvur turned pale, and trembled at the knees. 'It's a dying man, Father, thrown up by the sea! I wouldn't dare go near him!'

'Oh, hold your noise,' hissed Ketil. 'I suppose you'd sooner risk letting him die in the surf – and then he'd haunt us as long as we lived.' The old man went toward the noise. Kálvur followed him, a cable's length behind.

The cry was coming from a bank of foam on the east side of the bay. There were no words, only cries and groans. Ketil supposed it must be some foreigner who was thrown ashore, and he shouted into the foam, in a mixture of Danish and Faroese, 'Hang on, my friend, I can hear you, and I'm on my way to help!' So Ketil dived into the foam, threatening and urging Kálvur to follow him. But in the foam bank they fell to squabbling, for Kálvur was so frightened that sometimes he lost his grip, and sometimes he fell over, while they were carrying the man out. Ketil begged the man not to take it ill. They were trying to help him, but his son was so young – 'and he sometimes makes mistakes through lack of experience.'

When they emerged, they saw that it was Klávus they had rescued, and they stood there disconcerted. 'Lord bless us, Klávus. Whatever happened to you?' They could see that he had broken his leg.

But Klávus said nothing about that. He was fussing about a beast, The Beast, which had risen up out of the sea, and that now, the end of the world was close at hand.

'No need to talk like that,' Ketil consoled him. 'You've broken your leg, and now we're going to look after you. No Beast has risen up. As for the end of the world, that rests in God's hands, and when it does come, it'll be no good flinching from it.'

Then Klávus raised himself from the grass on his elbow, and stared wild-eyed down towards the foam bank. 'It has, it has! The Beast has risen up! It's down there in that foam bank.

I fell over it and I heard it snorting.' He crossed himself, with both hands, and fell back onto the grass, weeping bitterly.

Ketil stood there thinking it out. He must have encountered something in there. The old man became more and more inquisitive. 'Klávus,' he said, 'just calm down now, and tell me what it was you felt. What was it like? Was it big, and was it alive?'

But Klávus was utterly distraught, and fussed the whole time about how the sun would now fall from the heavens, and the moon would be darkened, and how it would rain brimstone. 'And oh, that lovely plank of mine – I was going to put it to ever such a good use – and now all this is coming to pass!'

Ketil stood digging his fingers into his beard, and looking seriously at the foam bank. He had no desire to step into it before he got to know what it was that Klávus was fussing about. It might be something that he could put to good use. He took his gun and loaded it. 'It can't be as frightful as all that,' he thought. And he went down.

Kálvur followed anxiously behind, creeping along with his arms full of stones, and crouched behind a boulder.

Ketil stuck the muzzle of the gun into the foam, rooted around, and went forwards. But then he turned back again. It was a serious matter going in, because the foam was so deep that you couldn't see a thing, and Klávus was lying there on the grass groaning away in the utmost distress. But then he became eager once again, for he thought that perhaps there was a good catch, and he turned back in once more. He put one hand to his nose, so that he could breathe, while in the other he held his gun, and felt his way forwards.

Now he got right into the cleft, as far as he dared go toward the breakers. With the muzzle of the gun he felt something soft, which moved. Before he thought what he was doing, he took the gun in both hands and fired. The barrel was so short, the recoil knocked him over on his back when it went off. And as he lay there, he began to have misgivings. 'What was it I felt, now?' he asked himself. 'Perhaps it was a man.' And he was so startled, that he burst out crying, 'Oh, Jesus have mercy on me!'

You would have thought that Kálvur had grown wings, the way he flung the stones away from him and fled from the beach blubbering. Klávus began to sing the hymn, 'To Thy mercy do I fly.'

Ketil lay there a little while recovering his breath. Then he got up again. There was nothing to be done about it; he had not had any evil intentions – and it was God's hand at work, if he had wounded a man. But he must know what had happened, so he groped his way forward. First he encountered a head, then a neck behind it, and a flank with a wound in it, through which warm blood was oozing. At last he found a fin. 'Thank God,' he said, 'it's only a seal!'

Gradually, it dawned on him that he had made a good kill. He felt a sudden glow of pride, and at once his manner became playful. As he waded out of the foam bank again, he started singing the ballad of 'Regin the Smith':

> High in the air his pinions spread,
>> But low his body hung;
> And Sjúrður faced that dragon fierce
>> And his sword against him swung.

Kálvur was at this moment running at top speed up the hill-side. Ketil cupped his hands in front of his mouth and shouted to him to come down again. 'I've shot a seal!'

When Klávus heard about the seal, he raised himself up from the grass a little again. Now he piped another tune. His lower lip fell, and he stopped crossing himself. 'Well, I'm damned,' he said, 'they've pulled off something this time.'

When they were dragging the seal well above high-water mark, it was all very jolly. Ketil laughed so much that every now and then he had to stop pulling. He thought about Klávus, who lay there with his broken leg, devouring the seal with his eyes. 'He's never had such a mortification in all his born days,' Ketil thought.

Now they had the job of getting Klávus home. The seal would have to wait, and they would come back for it later.

Kálvur said, 'There's no other way but taking turns carrying him on our backs.'

'We wouldn't get far with him that way,' replied Ketil. 'Carrying a burden that way is very hard going. We need to fix him in some way so that we can carry him between us.'

'It's a shame about my plank,' Klávus groaned. 'Now, it's going to be left lying out here. It'll be long enough before I can come over here again to fetch it in, I should think.'

'We'll come across this evening, and take it to your storehouse.'

'Thank you very much; but the storehouse is locked up.'

They did not reply to this one. If Klávus was afraid to let the key out of his hands for that brief length of time, his plank could stay where it was.

'I suppose I couldn't sit on the plank while you carried me? I think it would be easier for you.'

'We could manage your weight well enough that way,' said Ketil. 'But could you bear to sit there on the plank, with your broken leg?'

'Yes, why not? I should think I could.'

When they had got Klávus on the plank, and were ready to set off, he said to Kálvur, 'Just pass me my catfish, old chap, and I'll carry it in my hand. You can fetch the bits of wood home for me when you come out here again.' Then they set off.

When they reached Klávus's storehouse, they were ready to drop with exhaustion. Klávus asked them to carry him up to the door, as he was used to the lock and could lock it up himself. So they laid Klávus down on the grass and put the plank inside.

'There should be one of those carrying frames we use for big stones, somewhere in there,' said Klávus. 'Can you see it? It would be best if I sat in that, and it would make it easier for you.'

Ketil and Kálvur agreed that this would be best. Klávus was extremely accommodating, it had to be admitted; he sat exactly as they wanted him to sit. But he would not let the catfish out of his hands. 'It doesn't do to come home without bringing something back for supper,' he remarked.

There was no more talk on the way home. Ketil and Kálvur became very weary, taking turns carrying the heavy burden. And by degrees, Klávus's injury became more and more painful. A couple of times they had to stop and give him water, for he nearly fainted when Kálvur stumbled with him, and his broken leg jarred on the ground.

When they reached the village, Klávus asked them, 'How

do you think the seal ought to be shared, seeing it was I who found him in the first place?'

But Ketil and Kálvur replied that they did not intend to share it. 'We intend to keep that seal for ourselves.'

Then they carried Klávus to his house.

CHAPTER FOUR

Ketil's wife was standing in the doorway when the two came back from Klávus's house. She had tears in her eyes and a handkerchief in her hand. 'Lord have mercy on us,' she said, 'you didn't bring him back dead?'

'No, thank the Lord, he's not dead ... he was just so greedy to lay his hands on other folk's property, that his shanks gave way under him ... and so he became a burden to others.'

When she saw they were laughing, she recovered her voice, and her face broadened into laughter. 'Good for you!' she said. She gave Ketil a dig in the ribs. 'Klávus's wife was ever so hoity-toity with me this morning – wrinkled her nose, and stuck it in the air. "Well, well, how empty your house is this morning!" she said, and laughed in a scornful way.'

Kálvur was desperately hungry now he had got home, and he began to bellow for food.

'Don't you think you ought to change into dry things before you eat?' asked his mother.

'No, I'm not bothered about that, but I'm so hungry I could die!' And he twisted up his face and whimpered.

The old woman went to fetch the pot. 'Lord preserve us,' she said, 'are you going to let the whole lane hear how hungry you are, now you have got home?'

'I'll slip across and see the lads,' said Ketil. 'I might be able to get them to go over to West Bay to fetch in our catch.'

A little afterwards, he came back and sat himself heavily down by the fire to dry his feet. He sat there frowning and breathing hard into his beard.

His wife took a pair of stockings from the fireplace and gave them to him. 'Oh dear, I remember now, there are holes in the heels – I'll darn them right away,' she said.

'No, let me.'

'Come here, let me do it.'

They both pulled at the stockings, but Ketil won.

By this time, Kálvur was well fed, and was lying along the bench on his back, asleep.

Ketil's darning came to nothing, for he was in such a bad mood that his wool broke.

His wife walked away, a little shamefaced, and rooted around in the kitchen. Then she came back to him, laid her hand on his knee, and said very gently, 'It was a shame, my dear, to give you stockings with holes in when you've been so hard at work in the open. Now you're ruining the darning wool, while you sit there puffing and blowing.'

Ketil turned his head and spat under the bench. 'A pair of stockings out of heel? – that's not the damn trouble. There's far worse than that. We've got five great oafs of sons living around us, and here I am in my seventieth year, but I have to reckon myself the only man among the lot.'

'What did the lads say?'

'What did they say? Scorn was all I got – they laughed at me for going out and gathering all that rubbish together.'

'Did you tell them about the seal?'

'Yes. They said it was just like me to go and shoot a poxy old seal.'

'Wouldn't they go over to West Bay and fetch it in for you?'

'No. They would come for a bit in the morning to help me with it for part of the way, but they weren't going to make themselves a laughing-stock by hauling such a thing through the village.'

'Well, I don't know!' said his wife haughtily. 'There's no limit to their airs and graces since they left this house! Now they're too proud to fetch a bit of fish home! No, I've said it a hundred times before: it's those wives of theirs, the hussies, that are ruining them. I don't know what daft notions they've got hold of – the sort of nonsense they grew up with in the big villages. Now they're married, they're all wanting to ape the wealthy folk, running to the shops, and sitting around in their Sunday best, thinking they can make a living by wrapping themselves up in their rags all day long. And never are they more self-important than when they haven't got a chemmy to cover their bottoms with.'

Ketil ate his supper in silence, without looking up. When he had finished, he went into the byre, and came back with a handful of hay. Then he sat down by the fire to dry the inside of his shoes.

'Are you putting your shoes on again?' asked his wife. 'Aren't you ready for a bit of rest yet?'

'I think my first rest will be in the churchyard. I must try and struggle back to West Bay, now that I've had something to eat. It's no good getting something unless you fetch it home.'

The old woman stared at him. 'You must be out of your mind. Do you think an old fellow like you can stand being out at West Bay for a second night in succession?'

'It's no use talking about what I can stand. Do you suppose that the District Sheriff will ask what I can stand, when he comes to demand payment of that bill for the whale meat? All my life I've had to do more than I could stand, and I'll do it tonight as well. But I don't know what the world's coming to. Those who do least, live best.'

His wife made no answer, but sat down and changed her shoes, put on a clean pair of pattens, and bound her head with a shawl. 'Now I'm going over to the pastor's, to borrow a horse and a crook-saddle. You hang those shoes of yours up again, now, and go and lie down. You can go fetch your kill at first light tomorrow morning. This time, it's going to be the way I say it.'

Ketil's troubled face cleared, and he slapped his wife on the shoulder. 'Old girl, you're a brick,' he said. 'Damn me if I'd swap you for any of the younger lot, prettier though they may be.'

The pastor lent them the horse very willingly. He was both kindly and courteous, and asked how things had gone.

'God be praised, very well,' said Ketil's wife, and with the eloquence of Ecclesiasticus, she told him what they had got.

'So, you've shot a seal, have you?' said the pastor. 'I should be very glad to buy the skin.'

This was indeed good news to carry home.

Before first light the following morning, the old couple began to squabble in bed. She wanted to get up and make a cup of coffee for them before they went off.

'You just lie there, my dear, it's better for the men to get up first,' said Ketil.

She would not hear of this. She stuck her feet out from under the bedclothes and tried to get up. But then he took hold of her and put her back again. 'This time, it's going to be the way I say it,' he said. Then he went to get the fire ablaze.

They could not get Kálvur to wake up. They talked kindly to him, shook him, shouted at him and pinched him, but with no result. Kálvur merely grumbled ill-humouredly, and rolled himself up in the bedclothes in a deep and noisy sleep. 'Blast the fellow!' burst out Ketil, and he took a wet cloth and wiped it across his son's face.

Then Kálvur cried, and the old woman swept out of bed like a whirlwind. 'Let my poor boy alone!' she said. 'If you bully him any more, you'll be sorry for it.' And she picked up her loom stick. 'I thought all the time that you'd create trouble when you got up this morning.'

'All right, all right,' muttered Ketil, giving up the struggle, and starting to put on his shoes.

His wife did the same – put on her shoes. She dressed herself, and wound a shawl around her head. Then she set about preparing food.

Ketil stared at her. 'Where are you off to so early?' he asked.

Then she laughed at him, almost with the tone of a young girl. 'I'm coming with you,' she said. 'Do you suppose I'm going to let you go off by yourself in the middle of the night?'

'You can't mean it. Are you getting up this early to go over to West Bay with me?'

'Of course. Does it surprise you if I want to slip out and get a breath of fresh air?' She came with half a loaf of ember-baked bread for him. 'What do you want with this?' she asked.

'Give me a lump of mutton dripping.'

So they ate bread and dripping, drank milk-and-water with it, and when they had finished, they folded their hands together and gave thanks to God for their meal.

'There's no harm in leaving Kálvur lying here by himself, is there?' said the old woman.

'No, he'll surely want to sleep on until it's fully light. And he isn't a babe in arms.'

So they harnessed the horse and set off in fine weather. The ground was firm and frozen. All the stars were twinkling, and in the middle of the sky, an aurora was hanging in great long folds. The heavens seemed immense. The streams seemed to ring out like bells, so still it was at this hour. The horse stamped impatiently.

The old folk steeled themselves to their task, and felt young again in spirit. Ketil wanted his wife to get up and ride, but she refused until they were past the infield wall. 'I wouldn't dare to sit astride a horse anywhere where folks might see me,' she said.

'Don't be so silly, talking like that. Your legs are no uglier than anyone else's, and these days, every woman's skirt shows half her thigh.'

When Kálvur woke again, as it was beginning to get light, he started to shout for breakfast. He was really hungry, he said.

When he got no answer, he bellowed and thumped on the panel. But everything was quiet, except that the hens sitting on the crossbeam began to cackle. So he leapt out of bed and flung open the kitchen door, and shouted, 'Why can't you answer me?' But he retreated and stiffened himself when he found that the house lay dark and empty. As nimbly as a trout he sprang back into bed and wrapped himself up in the bedclothes. He stared into the dark room, and every time he heard the slightest noise, he would shiver to the roots of his hair, and vow to sin no more.

As he lay there, the door opened and someone came in. Then he got his courage back again. 'Come in!' he shouted.

'What did you say?' was the reply.

'Come in here,' he called out again.

It was Klávus's daughter.

'Oh, it's you. I thought it was Mother,' stammered Kálvur, disappointed, from the semi-darkness.

'Yes, I came to beg a kindling. Our fire has burned right out.'

'Nobody's in but me. I don't know where the others are.'

'They went off somewhere. I saw them going up the lane with a horse.'

'With a horse? ... Can't you stay here until it's full daylight? I get so nervous.'

Yes, she could do that right enough. 'I'll go and sit by the kitchen fire, while you get dressed.'

When Kálvur was dressed, he went into the kitchen and sat at the other side of the fireplace. For a long time they sat in silence, giggling quietly and looking down at the floor.

Then Kálvur said, 'Isn't it funny, our being alone in the house; don't you think so?'

Yes, she thought so too. Then they sat silent again, stroking the corners of the fireplace.

Then Kálvur asked, 'How's your father doing?'

'Fairly well, but he has to lie there so long. And now we've nobody who can get any food for the household. I don't know what we shall do – there isn't enough for a supper left in the house now.'

'That's a real shame for you,' stuttered Kálvur, and he went around to the other side of the fire-place. 'Come and have a cuddle,' he said.

He tried to take hold of her around the waist, but she slipped free. 'Not unless you give me a potful of whale meat,' she said.

'That won't stand in our way!' said Kálvur, and he made for the larder.

She sat down again, shocked at herself. What she had done was a shame and a sin. But no one would ever know. Kálvur was not so daft that he would tell anyone. And whale meat was good to have; besides, there were many ways of getting a meal that were more trouble than cuddling Kálvur for a bit. Moreover, he would not be excessively demanding. She began to laugh.

Klávus lay humbly on his bed, thinking most of the time about God, and about the seal. Life was a burden to him now, he felt exhausted, and he heaved great sighs.

His wife came in and asked how things were going.

'Oh, don't talk about it,' he answered. 'I'm stranded on an ebb tide, my dear, and I'm no use for anything. But leave my room, wife, and shut my door, for I want to be alone in God's presence for this hour.' And he turned his face to the wall, for he was weeping.

'If only I had enough to live on,' he moaned, 'I wouldn't have any need to go around stealing, and everyone's food supplies would be safe as far as I was concerned. For when have I ever done these things by evil intent? Never. But bowed down with troubles, and crushed in spirit, I have wandered among the storehouses at night, and every night I have prayed that this should be the last time I did this thing. And every time I have tasted what was another man's, I have remembered faithfully to pray to Heaven to restore him tenfold. What I have borne home has little benefited me, for I lie here, worn out, old before my time. But what was there to do? That unendurable hunger! And never did any help come to me. Some men had sons, and others had sons-in-law. Those are the ones they can thank that they are able to tread in lawful paths. We have only one miserable daughter, and how can she help us, poor thing?'

He wept, and bade the Lord take him from the world. He had nothing to live for, he was guided by Mammon. But then he noticed the smell of his supper – whale meat! – and the will to live returned to him. 'The soil's produce is good, and God be thanked for it,' he said, 'but to eat it always – there's no strength in it.'

But where could the supper have come from? 'Come in here, my girl!' he called to his daughter.

She came.

'Where did you get the supper from, my child?'

'We ... we got it ... Ketil gave it to us.'

'I see.' He stared at the girl. She blushed, and slipped away. 'Ah, Christ have mercy on me,' he said, 'are you now doing the same? ... you, a mere child? The lucky ones are those who escape from this vale of misery, and safe and sound reach the gates of Heaven.'

Quite early in the morning, the infield wall was alive with grandchildren, sitting and waiting for the old folk coming back with the catch. As soon as they came in sight, the whole swarm rushed up toward them, yelling and shouting. 'Hurrah, here they come!' 'Grandad, give me a bit of wood to make some pattens!' 'Grandad, give me a bit of wood for a boat!' 'Grandma, give me a fish!' The youngest ones came tottering behind, as bow-legged as water beetles, calling out, 'Ah, Grandad, give us some seal, give us some seal!' They crowded up so much that the old woman had to pick up a stick to drive them away from the load.

When they came to the infield wall, the children ran on ahead towards the village, calling out that Grandad and Grandma had come back from West Bay with all sorts of delightful things. Folk swarmed to the windows and on to the stairways to look at them and laugh. 'Ketil's wife doesn't relish the children shouting her arrival all around the place,' they said. 'Look at the way she's trying to hide her face!'

When the old folk got back to their house, all their daughters-in-law were sitting on the bench. Some had pails with them, and others had baskets. They'd just been to the shop, and had dropped in as they passed. 'Thought it would be very nice to have a fish, now that the men were not at sea.'

Their sons strolled along the lane, hands in pockets. They stuck their heads in at the door. 'Fine load of muck you've gathered together there, Father,' they said. Then they spat and went.

The old folk were speechless, and as grim as an avalanche. But their daughters-in-law still sat there. When Ketil had carried everything in and heaped it on the floor, they devoured it with their eyes, while the children fell to grovelling among the things.

Ketil said to them, 'Yes, you can have a few heads and suchlike, but we intend to sell the fish.'

Their faces fell, and they started whispering to one another about cods' heads. They sat erect and fuming.

Ketil's wife weakened. It was the poor children she was sorry for. 'Yes, yes, maybe you can take a fish along, so you've something to put in the pot,' she said.

When they left, there was no more than a single good cooking left on the floor. There was nothing to sell.

'So much for that,' snorted Ketil. Dead tired, he sat back by the fireplace and took his shoes off.

'Yes,' hissed his wife, 'those painted baggages came fast enough. When food comes so near to them they can goggle at it, they can do that; but go and get some for themselves – they're too delicately reared for such a thing.'

They got 12 kroner from the priest for the seal-skin.

In the evening, Ketil went over to see Klávus. 'He could easily let me have that plank he found. And I could give him a little something in return,' he said. 'They aren't so very well off, I shouldn't think.'

Klávus looked well enough. 'But I have to lie here so long, and I'm no good for anything as long as I'm on my back.'

'Too true, too true,' said Ketil, 'but there was one thing I wanted to ask you. Would you let me have that plank of yours? And in exchange, we could let you have a bit of good stuff for your supper.'

Klávus thought this was all very well. 'But it's a bit rash to let a plank like that one pass out of your hands, when you might have good use for it later on.'

'Very true, very true. I just thought I'd ask,' said Ketil.

'Yes, I shan't want to part with that,' answered Klávus.

As Ketil was leaving, Klávus's wife said to him, 'I should like to thank you for what you gave our daughter this morning. It came in very handy.'

'What was that?' asked Ketil.

'Oh, didn't you know about it? It was a potful of whale meat and blubber.'

'No, I didn't know about it, but there's nothing to thank us for. You're very welcome.' And then he went home again.

'Well, did you get the plank?' asked his wife.

'Did I as hell get the plank! He's lying there fat and happy in his bed, and eating our whale meat, so he's got no pressing need to part with his plank. But what do you think you're doing, flinging whale meat all around the village? Am I such a brisk old chap that I'm likely to fetch home another lot?'

'What's that you say? Have they had some of our meat?' said his wife, astonished. 'Kálvur, did you take some up to them?'

'Me? No,' said Kálvur. 'I haven't taken them any meat.'

'Yes, you must have. They said themselves that they got it this morning. Unless they stole it, the scum.'

Then it came out that Kálvur *had* given them the meat.

'Are you in your right mind, lad? Why did you do a thing like that?' demanded Ketil.

Then Kálvur straightened himself up, and put a bold face on the matter. 'Yes, I am in my right mind. I gave Klávus's daughter some whale meat – because she's my girl.'

'Well, well, lad, so she's your girl, is she?' laughed Ketil. 'And what do you do with her, may I venture to ask?'

'I shan't tell you,' said Kálvur, drawing himself up and turning obstinate. 'You're not going to laugh at me – I'm not a little boy any longer.' He took a pipe out of his pocket and lit up. 'I'm a grown man now.'

The evening ended in high merriment at Ketil's house.

The third day after this, Ketil again went over to Klávus's house and talked about the plank. But it was no use. Klávus mumbled about having the whole seal, or a couple of hundredweight of whale meat in exchange, and that was sheer robbery.

When Ketil got home again, the old folk told Kálvur in the strictest terms that he was not to give any more meat away until they had got the plank.

'For as long as he's got a mouthful left, he won't let it go, you see.'

The seventh day Klávus again refused.

'Well, well, I just thought I'd ask,' said Ketil.

'Yes, I shan't want to part with that,' answered Klávus.

But on the twelfth day, Ketil succeeded. 'Don't talk to me about whale meat,' begged Klávus. 'You'll drive me out of my mind. I've not tasted any good red meat for nine days now. Give me a hundredweight of whale meat, and you can have the plank right away.'

So Ketil settled down to carve an oar.

CHAPTER FIVE

It was a cold morning, and snow was lying on the hills. Ketil sat in front of the boathouse, caulking the seams of his boat.

About breakfast time Tummas arrived, bareheaded, and with his clenched fists thrust into his pockets. He draped himself over the boathouse door and remained standing there. His jaws revolved like millstones, and the pavement around him became dark with tobacco spit.

Tummas was a young man. He had a wife and children, and a house bought with a savings-bank mortgage, and that was all. In the summer he went fishing.

'You're tough all right,' said Tummas admiringly. 'Already out of bed and making your boat tight. You put us young men to shame.'

'It doesn't really amount to much, the pottering about I do,' snorted Ketil. 'It's just that we older folk aren't accustomed to hang about doing nothing, my friend.'

'What are you going to do with that boat when you've put in all this work on it – sell it?'

'Ho-ho! Sell it?' laughed Ketil. 'This is a fine thing to sell. Who do you think would buy this old tub?'

There was no more talk than this, but Tummas did a fair amount of guessing, and went the rounds of the village, full of news. 'Ketil's going to sell that old wreck of a boat of his. He got up before daybreak this morning to caulk her seams.'

Men, newly out of bed, sat down with stockings around their ankles, chewing. They scratched their heads and swore. 'Ketil, the old rogue, he'd find a way of making money if you put him on a tide-washed skerry without a blade of grass. You don't know what he's going to get for it – and who's going to buy it?'

'Don't ask me,' replied Tummas. 'It could be one of the sloop owners. It'd be good enough for a ship's boat, they'd think. Don't you reckon he could get a hundred kroner for it?'

Tummas had not gone far around the village, before the details about the shipowner and the hundred kroner were no longer conjecture, but sober fact. They even named the shipowner who was to buy the boat.

Before very long, Tummas had been around the village, and had come back to the boathouse. Then he stuck his legs out, and leaned spine and rear quarters against the boathouse door, and let his pipe weigh his head forwards over his chest. He stood in this way, half dozing.

Other people arrived, strolling in from all over the village, to the boathouse. Some of them were carrying tools, and were on their way to work, but had come around this way before they went off. Others had neither tools nor plans, but were just strolling around, taking it easy for the five months until they went off with the fishing boats again.

Jóhan stood there, and straightened his back. 'You're a sly old hound, Ketil, the way you turn everything to account,' he jeered. 'Are you going to get some service out of that leaky old tub now? The folk that sail in that one will have a fine craft underneath them!'

Ketil glanced up and spat, but said nothing. Jóhan slapped his shoulders to warm himself, and laughed, well content to have dared to make a bit of fun out of Ketil. But no, it was silly for him to hang around here, he was on his way to Dale Head to do a job there. He took his spade on his shoulder and went off. His wife was lying in with her ninth. Two grown lads of his were just at this moment coming through the gate into the infield. They were carrying creels, and had been out stealing peat.

The others stood silently, unwilling to mock an old man as Jóhan had done. They had just come across to see with their own eyes if it was true what Tummas had said, that he was converting this discarded boat into a ship's boat. They stood there amazed, looking at one another and shaking their heads. Some of them swore.

They began to talk about other things, and now about the bad times. 'Damned hard times. Seven hundred kroner – a deckhand won't get any more than that. How are folk going to pay their way?'

Then Jóhan came back with the spade over his shoulder.

'What, didn't you go to Dale Head, then?' someone asked him. No. He had met some people on the way, and the time had just slipped away. 'And now it's so near lunch time, it's not worth going over there,' he explained. He began to talk with the others about how bad the times were.

Now Ketil placed his tar-pot under the boat, wiped his hands on his trousers, and joined the others. He pulled an ember-baked loaf out of a glove he had pushed under his trouser belt, and settled down with them to eat it.

They asked him what he thought of the bad times. He replied that he didn't know a great deal about these things – he wasn't a very clever man, and he'd never been to school. 'But I can tell you that good health is everything, my friends. This I *do* know, that if God only grants that, one can do almost anything else. And, thank God, all of us who went out to the fishing this spring have come back safe and sound. Neither have we had war or crop failure in our part of the world.' Then he fell silent, and ate his bread.

An uneasiness spread around the flock. Their faces darkened, and they seemed to want to conceal any tools they had with them. They all gaped, and some time passed before anyone could find words in reply.

Then Jógvan burst out, 'Health is a good thing to have, all right, but damn it, you can't eat it ... when there's nothing to be earned.'

'I don't see how that can be,' answered Ketil mildly. 'We all have our land to till, and a boat.'

Then one of them gave a sharp laugh. 'Eat earth, yes.'

'And fish that don't take your hook,' added another.

'I don't know,' answered Ketil, stuffing himself with his bread. 'The old folks used to say that anyone who had a cow in his house wouldn't starve. If we till our land, we can raise potatoes and barley. If you keep yourself in food, and perhaps get a bit of money from boat-fishing while you're at home, you can keep going. We have peat. That way, you can make your fishery earnings stretch out perfectly well ...' He intended to say more, but then he noticed that nobody was left there in the boat-house. So he carried on repairing his boat.

The following morning Ketil and Kálvur went out fishing. They sat and bickered.

'Shame on you,' said Ketil, 'sitting there laughing while I'm struggling away teaching you about the fishing grounds. In my young days there was no giggling when older men were teaching the younger ones. Everyone did his best to learn as much as he could, so that he could catch the most fish, and measure himself satisfactorily against other men.'

'No, I wasn't laughing at you, Father, I was laughing at the moon – it's so strange that it should be in the sky during the day, when it isn't needed.'

'My dear lad,' replied Ketil scornfully, 'are you sitting there laughing at the moon, when I'm trying to give you the wisdom of a man?'

'Yes, but why doesn't God make the moon shine at night instead of wasting its light in the daytime?'

'What a fellow!' scolded Ketil. 'If you've started courting, you've got to think about setting up your own household. Do you think you can feed a wife and children by laughing at the moon?'

Kálvur blushed, and stroked the oarlock. He thought it was a bit improper of his father to start talking about children the very moment he had started courting. He thought that people didn't think about such things until they were married. 'I can earn my living,' he said, 'even if I don't know all these little fishing grounds. I can go with a ship!'

'The pity of it is, deckhands *don't* need to know the village fishing grounds,' said his father. 'I don't know what the world's coming to. In the old days it would have been reckoned shameful not to know your way round the sea near your own village. For example, when folk got together at a whale hunt, or at some festivity, that's what the talk would be about. And those who didn't know anything would leave the talking to those who did. But now it seems that the ones who carry their heads highest and have most to say are those who know nothing.'

Then they pulled in their fishing line and rowed the boat against the current, which had carried them away from the tiny fishing ground.

'We didn't get anything,' said Kálvur. 'It won't be any use rowing back again.'

'Oh, yes, we'll try once again, and I'll bring the boat just a shade further over,' replied his father.

This time they got some fish. When fish were flopping about in the bottom of the boat, it cheered the two of them up a good deal. Kálvur stood there excitedly hauling them in.

Every time his son hooked a fish, Ketil said, 'Huh, just pull it in, lad, just pull it in.' He talked in a confidential tone, as if he were afraid someone would overhear them and get envious. 'I think you're doing well,' he told Kálvur, laughing. 'You've got fishing luck.' He sat ruminating, while he pulled at the oars. 'Maybe he will become a fisherman – he's got the luck for it. So he'd be as much use as many another man with a better headpiece. And what use are their brains to many of them? They just sit and pore over books, and hanker after every possible thing that folk have in other places, instead of doing something useful at home.'

They did well at the fishing that day.

In the evening, when they rowed home again, they were happy and joking, and passed the time in singing. Kálvur imitated the call of the eider duck. When they neared land, however, Ketil bade him guard his tongue. 'No chattering when we go ashore. And if anyone asks you about anything, tell them as little as you can.'

As they came in, men were standing and watching from the boathouses.

'Did you get a good catch today, old fellow?' asked someone. And they laughed.

'No, just a few,' replied the old man.

Kálvur stepped ashore to hold the boat. Ketil threw the fish out of the boat. But first he flung ashore an oilskin jacket.

'Not much flesh on that one,' said one of the men, laughing.

The old man did not answer, but took up an old buoy they had found, and flung that ashore.

'Well, you can soon fill your damn boat with that sort of rubbish,' said another bystander.

But then the fish started to come. 'Damn me, if they haven't had a bite or two,' said another. The old man threw out the fish two by two. The men by the boathouses stopped talking and started counting. When Ketil had thrown out twenty, their eyes began to goggle and one of them said, 'They've had a good day.'

'Yes,' drawled one of the others, 'but if a single boat does get a few fish in a whole day's fishing, so what?' But the men disappeared.

Next morning there was good weather again, and Ketil and Kálvur set off from the shore as soon as it was light. When they had passed the skerries, they saw eight motorboats following them, foaming at the bows. The men were sitting in them, their elbows on their knees, smoking their pipes, while the motors throbbed away. The ones who passed nearest to them turned and laughed at Ketil and Kálvur, who were sweating away at the oarlocks.

That day they caught nothing; the sky became murky and the sea rather rough. The second day, the weather improved, but the boats still caught nothing. The third day, Ketil and Kálvur were alone again. Their catch was only a small one, but it included a halibut, which they sold, and got a few kroner for.

They continued fishing all week, and earned nearly forty kroner. This was a good week, Ketil reckoned. But Kálvur made a sour face over it, he was so exhausted. 'We should have had a motor – then it would have been child's play to go fishing, and we could have reached the farther fishing grounds,' he said.

Ketil laughed. 'Oh yes, I agree with you. If we had had a motor, we wouldn't have gone to the nearer grounds. The other boats didn't, did they?

Then the currents became stronger and the weather stormy, so they had to stay ashore.

Klávus was back on his feet again. He came over to Ketil's house and sat down to gossip. He was very serious this evening. The End was near now, he said, and he talked of the Lamb, that walked and grazed on the heavenly pastures, and had all things in abundance. 'And here I sit, a sinful man, with a broken leg, and hungry.' But then everyone jumped, for he sprang up from the bench onto the floor, shouting, 'Hell and damnation!' The cause of all this was a hen which was sitting on the beam above him, and which muted right down his neck.

Ketil's wife apologised to him. She was usually careful to keep the hens from getting so far over, but just now she had forgotten to do this. But Klávus had been put off conversation, and went.

The others laughed at him when he had gone. 'But it's a shame for the poor creature,' said Ketil. 'His future son-in-law ought to take them over a cod, I think.'

'Yes, certainly,' said Kálvur eagerly. 'I'd be the best one to do that.' So he went.

Just at that moment, at Klávus's, they were sitting down to supper: salt and potatoes. But when the codfish came, they left the table and began cooking once again.

'I heard some noise in your byre,' said Kálvur. 'I suppose your cow can't have broken loose?'

'It could very well be,' replied Klávus's wife. 'Do please go and have a look, my girl. And you, Kálvur, go along with her.' This he was quite willing to do.

When they were outside the door, Kálvur said, 'That was just my trick. The cow isn't loose at all. I just said it to get you outside for a little bit of courting.'

'It was a good thing you did that,' she replied. 'I was just sitting there wondering how we could kill time until the cod was cooked.'

So they went into the byre.

When Kálvur came home, he was flinging his chest out and slamming the doors.

'You were a long time away. Were you eating up their cod for them?' asked his father.

'No, I was talking with my girl.'

'Oh yes, and what did you say to her?'

'People don't go telling what they say to their girls.'

'Oh, they don't, don't they? I suppose you didn't tell her the land-sightings and cross-bearings we used when we went to find the fishing grounds?'

Then Kálvur hung his head, and admitted that he *had* told her about them. 'Because you've got to talk about something when you're with your girl. But she won't repeat them, that I do know. She's more loyal than to do such a thing.'

His mother clapped her hands together and roared with laughter. 'God bless us, we've got a pretty lover here, who sits and talks about cross-bearings with his girlfriend. She must be a bit desperate for a man, if she didn't chase you out of the house.'

'I didn't only talk about cross-bearings. I ... I ... also told her that I loved her.'

'Well, and what did you do with her?' teased Ketil.

'Oh yes, you think I wouldn't dare to tell you! I took her around the waist and kissed her, several times. I know how many times, but I'm not going to tell you that.' And they could get no more out of him.

Soon after they had been sitting and teasing Kálvur, and making merry, in came the area rating officer. They stiffened and gazed at him.

No, it was only a little matter he had come about, he was

only dropping in for a moment. It was some rates arrears he was dealing with, and he happened to be passing by, so ...

'But we've paid our rates,' said both the old folk in one breath. 'Didn't you enter it up?'

'Oh, yes, it wasn't that I meant. There's no difficulty about *your* rates. There's no occasion to call about *them*, you know that. But you did so well at the fishing last week, perhaps you could spare a bit for one of your sons.'

Ketil and his wife stared at each other. 'Do they owe on their rates?'

'Oh, no, not exactly. It's just the eldest who has got a bit behindhand.'

'No, no,' answered Ketil feebly. 'I'm now a seventy-year-old man. The young fellows must pay their own rates. It's got to be that way now.'

'There's also this about it,' added his wife, 'that even if we did pay a few kroner, it wouldn't make any difference, because it can't be any trifling debt, since you've come to us about it.'

'Oh yes, it would help, however little it was,' said the man.

'Yes, but I don't think we can do anything about it,' answered Ketil. 'We have our own affairs to think about, and we've both got one foot in the grave.'

'Of course, of course, I can well understand that you might not be able to pay, for naturally you have your own expenses. It was just this, that if I got thirty kroner, then I ... wouldn't have to take anything out of his house.'

The old people felt as though they had been stabbed. 'Is our son going to be sold up?'

The area rating officer shrugged his shoulders and wriggled the whole of the upper part of his body. 'Yes, only too true, only too true. We don't want to harass folk like this, but what can one do? I go round the village to get a few oyru in now and then, but get nothing from one year's end to the next.'

Ketil went into the bedroom, and came back with three ten-kroner notes and pushed them forward as if in a daze. The rating officer took them and slipped away. Not a word more was said.

All this time Kálvur was asleep on the bench with a whole potful of porridge in his stomach.

That night, neither of the old folk could sleep, but they lay in one another's arms, weeping.

About four o'clock Ketil got up, bored with lying there sleepless. And there was, perhaps, a job he could put his hand to. For example, there was his new oilskin jacket that he had thrown off the previous evening, when he had come in from the sea – it ought to be hung up so that it would dry. He went out to his storehouse, taking a lamp in his hand.

When he got outside, he found the storehouse door open. He started, but then recalled that it must have been Kálvur who had left it open the previous evening when he went for the cod, and gave it no more thought. He put his lamp on the floor, picked up a lath and thrust it through the oilskin, and was going to hang it up on the eaves. Then he saw a man standing up on the beams, and he jumped with surprise. 'Jesus preserve us, which of God's creatures is out here so late?'

'Don't ask who it is, my friend,' replied Klávus from the beam, 'but praise your Maker that you are not in my place this night. Had not the Almighty been so strong, here I would have hung lifeless, like a child of perdition. I felt so crushed that I despaired, and crept up here to hang myself. Now I am saved, miraculously snatched from the edge of the abyss.'

'Yes, yes, Klávus. Come on down now and get back to bed. Next time, do your despairing in the daytime, and come over to my house and ask me for what you need.' So he gave him a few dried fish, and lit his way out through the door.

A little after Klávus had gone, Ketil began to wax furious. 'God help me, I'm not right in the head,' he shouted into the storehouse. 'People beg from my right hand and steal from my left. And I do nothing about it. No, I'm through with my easygoing ways.' He leaped out into the lane, picked up a stone and hurried through the yard. Now, by the living God, he would go and pull Klávus's house about his ears. It was a sin and a shame to have an old thief like him running round and doing just what he liked.

But when he came over to his house, a light was burning inside, and he saw Klávus sitting by the fire with a stone across his knees. He was pounding the dried fish to prepare it for eating – and peace and humility were in his face.

Then Ketil's wrath subsided, and he dropped the stone. 'But I'm going to give him a piece of my mind.' And he flung the door open, and stepped into the house like a whirlwind. 'Now you're sitting here all cosy and pleasant, you old parasite, it would be no sin to give you a damn good thrashing!'

Klávus looked up, with calm and peaceful eyes, and stared paternally at Ketil. In a low voice, he said, 'Guard your tongue, my friend, and remember the apostle's words, "Let your communication be yea, yea, and nay, nay; for whatsoever is more than these, cometh of evil". I tell you this as one that has a care for your soul.' He calmly tore a bit off the fish, and fell silent.

But Ketil was not in a mood to be easily pacified. He clenched his fist and shook it in front of Klávus's nose. 'I could grind you into the ground, you thief! And you dare to take God's words into your mouth!'

Then Klávus began to cry, and begged Ketil not to bring further calamity upon him. 'A sinner I am, and my burden of guilt is great. But the more I am forgiven, the more I will have to give thanks for. O, Ketil, my friend, forget not in your wrath, that no child of man has sat without food through Klávus wending his sinful way amongst them. Never shall it be said on the Morning of Resurrection that I have emptied the poor man's larder. Humbly have I slaked my hunger, where God's gifts were in overflowing abundance. Sheathe the sword of your wrath, and threaten me not with your fist, as if I were a wicked wretch.'

'Yes, Klávus,' said Ketil, 'you're a wretched fellow, I know that. But why didn't you come and tell me when you were in need?'

'Don't add stones to my burden, Ketil. The beggar's step is a very heavy one. Humbly I drink the cup that the Lord gives me, and look for no betterment before that of the Kingdom of Heaven.'

CHAPTER SIX

The following morning, Ketil's wife began to smarten herself up. Was she going out? Yes, she had to go to the shop. 'Now, do you need anything this morning? Are you coming along?' she said.

Ketil answered, 'Shall I now? There's always more than enough to do, but if it's any use to you, I'll come along.'

'Well, it will be useful, because it looks like we'll have indoor weather for some time, so we ought to get some wool home to get to work on. You don't get much for knitting up a sweater, but it's still better than sitting with your arms folded.'

'Yes, yes, you're right there.' Ketil put on his shoes, and off they went.

Ketil said, 'It's a perfect nuisance the way every penny we earn goes as quick as it comes. I want to get this whale meat bill settled, but the way it's going, nothing seems to do any good.'

'Don't talk about that. I can't even bear to *think* about it. I wish for once I could have my way with these trollops our lads have married. Then they wouldn't be going around in their silks and satins and sticking their noses in the air.'

They came to the only shop in the village.

'Good day.' The shopkeeper, an elderly bachelor, sat on a soapbox, with a cravat round his neck, singing an old Faroese ballad.

What did they want?

The old woman wanted an ounce of tea.

'You don't want a slice of cheese as well, I suppose?' asked the shopkeeper.

No, she didn't want any.

'That's all right. I only asked because the cheese is lying on the tea chest, and I had to move it anyway.'

Ketil wanted some nails for his boat.

Certainly, he could have some, the shopkeeper told him, scratching himself under his cravat. 'But just now I was so clumsy as to drop the packet of nails into the treacle barrel.' He looked above him. 'Maybe I could use these fire tongs hanging here, to pick them out again. He climbed up to the beam, and got the tongs, but slipped down, and ended with both arms in an open drawer full of flour. A sort of fine snowdrift filled the whole room.

'Have you hurt yourself?' asked the old folk.

'Hurt myself? Oh no, not at all. Now you can have your nails.'

The next thing they asked for was raw wool for knitting.

'Plenty of wool,' said the shopkeeper. He pulled a ladder down from the loft and climbed up through the trap door. 'It's only from people like you that I make a living. The youngsters won't deal with me. Every time a man gets married, that's the last I see of him in this shop – he's too high-and-mighty to trade with me. It's these wives of theirs, who've been in

Tórshavn and picked up daft notions. If they really were as fine as they pretend ...'

'I think we can agree with you there,' said Ketil. They got the sack of wool out through the door, Ketil took it up around his neck, and they left.

On the way home, they met one of their daughters-in-law.

'Good Lord,' she tittered, 'you're not reckoning on an early death, if you're hoping to knit up that great heap of wool you're carrying.'

'Perhaps a few other people ought to think the same,' snapped Ketil's wife.

'Yes, and what do you mean by that? Is it me you're getting at?' asked the daughter-in-law.

'If the cap fits, wear it,' answered Ketil's wife.

'The cap, what cap? Am I doing nothing, just because I don't knit sweaters? You old people reckon everyone's idle except yourselves.'

Ketil began to walk on again. 'Now then, no need to start an argument about it. Let's get home.'

But the old woman did not mean to give up. She enjoyed harping on this string. She set her things down and put her hands on her hips. 'We old folk think – oh, I don't know what to say about it, we don't know what to think. A vagabond like you, you dare to talk! What have you done, since you came to this village?'

'I've looked after my house.'

'You've looked after it, ha-ha! Yes, I must say, you've looked after it very well. So that, for instance, you're going to find yourself turned out of your house neck and crop before so very long. No, dolling yourself up, you can do that, and lie whining in childbed every year, you can do that too. But as for getting something to put into the mouths of the poor things you've brought into the world – you're too fine a lady to do that.'

'Impudent old cow! What can you blame me for?' said the daughter-in-law, stepping right up to her. 'I've not had more children than you've had yourself. And it's not my job to provide food for them, it's the man of the house that does that. I've not wasted what he's laid in, I can tell you that. But no, you're hot under the collar because I don't choose to live in a shack like you, and spend all my time in coarse work. If I'd done the same as you, not looked after my house, not kept myself looking decent, not brought up my children properly, I could easily have knitted sweaters and carried cow muck out to the fields as well. But I don't intend to do that. I didn't get married to live like one of the animals!'

Ketil's wife started to cry. 'Yes, yes, I've heard enough now. You say I've not looked after my house. I'd like to know who's done it better. Can anyone come in and seize any of *our* property for debt? Tell me that.'

'Yes, that's the thing you always come back with. But it's no wonder you're well off, if all you think of is a few scraps of food to put in your mouths, and you save every brass farthing to pay the rates with. We could do that too if we liked, but we don't want to. We want to live like human beings.'

'Rates, do you say? You've got the face to mention rates? It's us you've got to thank for not being turned out for being behind with your rates, let me tell you.'

'Turned out? We pay our taxes by banker's order, in instalments, through the Savings Bank. As for rates, we shan't pay those again. They've had a transfer order on the shipowner, and they won't get any more.'

'They certainly have had more – *we* paid for you.'

'We didn't ask you to pay anything. If you're so daft as to let the rating officer have money because he's too incompetent to collect it before the owner goes bankrupt, then do as you please!'

Ketil's wife fell abruptly silent, and went on her way.

'There she goes, the silly old goose, all hot and bothered, thinking everyone in the world's out of step except herself,' shouted the daughter-in-law after her, before going off.

When Ketil's wife got home, she found her husband setting up the spinning-wheel. She wept and dried her eyes on a corner of her shawl.

'I told you to leave her,' said Ketil, smiling down into his beard.

'So help me, if she puts her foot over my threshold again, she'll get a bucket of water thrown over her – that I've promised her this very day. But Ketil, you must go back to that rating officer straight away. He's cheated us, he has – if that hussy wasn't lying.'

Ketil stared. 'What did you say? Did the rating officer lie to us?'

'Yes, that daughter-in-law of ours said that they'd paid their rates, they'd got something from the owner, I don't know what it's called, one of these new things that's come out lately.'

The old man sprang up from the bench like a cork out of a bottle, and went over to his son's house. Perhaps the Lord was going to permit the thirty kroner to be recovered!

The son laughed when he heard the story. 'That rascal

of a rating officer! Has he been getting his claws into you? Just come over with me and I'll see you get every penny back from him.'

When they reached the rating officer's, they found the place in complete uproar. Everyone was running about shouting and clamouring. The rating officer's wife bade them come into the office to wait.

'There's such a fuss here today,' she said in a friendly way. 'He's had a letter returned that he has to sign. This office work makes him so wild he's not fit to be approached.' Her voice sank to a whisper. 'I'll tell you – the teacher used to write his letters for him, but today he refused to do it, and now my man's in a terrible mood, just for that reason. The trouble is, we've not paid the teacher his salary for the last seven months, and he's trying to get his own back this way. That's the way it is – first they get a big salary, and then they turn saucy afterwards. My man's always *signed* the letters himself, so I think it's mean of the teacher not to *write* them.' She sighed heavily, and left.

Then the rating officer came in, in his shirt-sleeves. His sweaty hair hung down in rats' tails, and his eyes were as red as a wizard's. A cat was sitting on the floor. It got a rap on the back of its neck. 'You know you oughtn't to be here in the office,' he told it.

'There was a little matter we wanted to clear up,' said Ketil.

'Yes, I suppose so, but you must wait a bit, till I've got this letter signed. I can't be in two places at once.' Then he took his ink-pot and pen, leaned over the desk, and took his bearings. The veins stood out on his forehead and his eyeballs started from their sockets. He frowned, gripped his lower lip between his teeth, and stabbed the pen in so much that the ink stood like a thick fog on the paper. When he had finished writing, he sat down for a minute to recover, and then asked them their business.

'Well, it's this,' said the son. 'You've conned my father into giving you money for rates which I've already paid ...'

'Oh well, that's easily put right – the money's lying right here. This is the point – I can't get on with this new system where you give me a letter from the owner. We old folk, we stick to coin of the realm as payment between one man and another. I've no experience of this new way – I haven't got any confidence in it.'

'You must get some. I want you to give my father his money back this minute.'

The rating officer went and fetched the thirty kroner. 'You must bear with me if I'm not at home with these newfangled ways,' he said.

'No,' said the eldest son. 'As long as you keep this job, you'll get no indulgence from me. Why did you take it on? Why are you old folk always pushing yourselves forward, when the truth is that times have changed so much in this country, that you're just left gaping?' Then father and son left with the thirty kroner.

When Ketil got back to his house, he took hold of his wife's arm and burst into song over his success. 'I've got the money back again, old girl,' he told her. 'That was a lucky row you stirred up!'

The indoor weather lasted for weeks, and they worked all the time on their spinning and knitting.

Kálvur railed at his parents and cried, because he had to

spin. 'It's a proper shame!' he said. 'How many of the other young men do you suppose stay at home spinning?'

'All of them,' Ketil assured him.

'Not a single one! And yesterday, when I was in the shop, they shouted *spinster!* after me, and laughed.'

'Well, we can't help that,' said the old folk. 'We can't keep you here just as an ornament. If you don't want to work, you'll have to join up with those who live by propping up boathouses or draping themselves over the shopkeeper's counter.'

But no, he didn't want to be driven out; he would rather spin.

One day, he came home from Klávus's full of excitement – now he was going to get married, he said. 'They've asked me whether I'll go to their house to live, because they're not able to run the house by themselves any longer.'

'You, get married?' said Ketil's wife, astonished. 'Then the fat would be in the fire.'

'Why?' asked Kálvur.

'Who would provide the food for the love nest?'

'I shall go fishing next spring,' said Kálvur. 'Klávus promised to ask a skipper to take me along.'

'Yes, you could do that as well as anyone else,' said Ketil.

But this notion displeased his wife. 'God preserve us from a fellow like you!' she said.

Then the eldest son entered and asked what they were talking about.

'It's this,' said Ketil's wife. 'The folk at Klávus's have been enticing Kálvur into marrying their daughter. But what I say is this – how *can* he think of providing for such a household?

He wants to go on a fishing boat, but what could he do there without bringing shame on himself?'

'Kálvur, let me tell you,' replied the eldest son, 'is better fitted to be a deckhand than either I or many another man.'

'That's strange,' said the old woman. 'What's the use of intelligence, then, if Kálvur, who lacks it, is as good as these others?'

'That I can't tell you. But for a deckhand, it's an advantage to have as little intelligence as possible. The man who thinks least is best off. It's preposterous, but true.'

'I don't know,' she replied. 'Young people nowadays are never satisfied; they always want more and more. They want everything that folk have overseas.'

'How?' asked the eldest son.

'Perhaps I don't express myself very well. But you all demand so much from life – you're never satisfied. In the old days, a poor man was content if he had something to eat and a roof over his head. Nowadays, everything has to be so high-and-mighty. Everything you set your minds on, you have to have, whether you can afford it or not ... And everyone's up to their eyebrows in debt ... A fat lot of use it is having schools, books and I don't know what! In the old days we used to be a lot more reasonable.'

The eldest son laughed. 'Yes, but debt doesn't arise because we ask too much of life, but because our earnings are so low. Everything has to be as good as it is overseas, you say. Why shouldn't we want to have it just as good as other folk? Have foreigners any special right to demand more from life than we do?'

'No, it would be good to have a comfortable life; but when we can't afford it, what then?'

'That's because we're so backward ...'

'Maybe so, but what can be done about that? If you're poor, you're poor. God disposes the riches of this world, and you can't thrust Him out of His place. Didn't you ever learn that at school?'

'I never learned that, no,' said the eldest son in a passionate tone. 'But we did learn to think of ourselves as men. We learned that life is more than dry bread, and we have learned to ask for more. It was useless for you to ask for more. Besides, you didn't dare to. Every time you had the impulse to raise your heads a little, you thought God would be angry and that Satan would be rubbing his hands over your covetousness.'

'I don't know how folks come to make these demands, when there's no supply.'

'There's no supply? What the hell are you talking about? The whole ocean is a pot that's chock-full of fish, and all you need is a ladle to fetch it out with. The only trouble is, it's such a damn long time before you can get your fingers on the handle.'

Up to now, Ketil had remained silent, carrying on with his spinning; but now he joined in. 'So those young men who hang around the lane ends are waiting for the ladle, are they?' he said.

'Yes, that's what they're waiting for, and they're ready to seize the handle, the moment the ladle comes.'

'Who's going to come along with this ladle and put it into your hands, may I venture to ask?' said Ketil.

'That they don't know, but they do know, every day more surely, that it *will* come. And they long for it, with such a yearning, that one day it *must* come, if the sky has to split to give birth to it.'

'Why don't you all grow potatoes while you're waiting? Then at least you'd have enough to eat.'

'Why weren't you a schoolteacher? Then you'd have had more to eat, and still been able to spin.'

'I don't know, but I had no special bent for book-learning. And in my young days, it was not thought very manly to be a teacher. That job was more for the feeble fellows, who wouldn't be able to stand the life of other men.'

'I can say just the same. I had no special bent for the land, and in my younger days, those who grew potatoes were reckoned effeminate. Then, the *fishing line* was reckoned to be everything. But now a change has come, and I and many others have done so badly by the fishing line, that if you live long enough, you may yet see our sons begin to grow potatoes again!'

'I don't know how it all is. Perhaps we're so foolish that we can't discuss these things properly.'

'I don't know whether you're foolish or wise, but you *are* old. So much has happened since you were young, that you hardly know where you stand – and then you go around prophesying hunger and ruination. Stop it; nothing's out of order – it's just a swing of the tide. Your tide has ebbed; now ours is flowing.'

The eldest son now left them. The old folk sat there frowning, and continued their work on the wool.

'Was he drunk, or why was he like that?' asked the old woman.

'I don't know, I don't know,' said Ketil impatiently. 'I can't make head or tail of things any more.' He hung the wool he had spun on the axle of the spinning wheel, and went out for a stroll in the fields.

During the night there was a storm, and piece after piece of the turf on the roof of Ketil's house was ripped off. The old man went around the village, waking up folk to come and help.

The middlemost son was annoyed at being awakened. 'Are you running around after your roof again? Put corrugated iron on your roof, and then we'll get a bit of peace at night! Fancy having a damn roof that you have to ask folk to sit and hold on to, every time there's a real use for it!'

The old men were the first on the spot, well clad, and armed with lines and hooks. They were serious and thoughtful. The younger ones hung around in the background, empty-handed. They did not care for this struggling with the storm, when they had their feet firmly on the ground.

Both the turf and its supporting birch bark had already been ripped off the gable, and some way in along the main roof. Some of the old men sat up there clinging on to the remainder. Every time a squall came sweeping down upon them, they flattened themselves against the roof and clung hard to the laths. Their knees became white, their jackets and beards flapping away in the wind, but they held on and saved the roof. Others carried up turf, spiked it together, and laid weighted lines over the top. Then everyone went home. 'But for all that, a turf roof's the best roof,' was the first thing they said when they had got warm again and recovered their powers of speech.

Kálvur was not up there saving the roof. 'I might get blown

away,' he thought, 'and then it would be bad, because folk would laugh at me.' He longed for the morning, when he would slip out and gather up the bits of birch bark that had been blown away. Birch bark was better to burn than anything else. It curled up, hissed, and smelled ever so good – and the smoke made you simply yearn for a woman.

Klávus was also out walking about that night, though he shook and quaked. 'Jesus have mercy on the poor man,' he cried out. 'He has to go in search of a morsel of food, by night as well as by day, and in bad weather as well as good.' He thought that at any time it might please Heaven to rip the roof off a storehouse on such a night as this. And if a pair of dried cod, or a side of dried lamb, or such like should happen to fall outside, then he could just as properly take it home as if the birds of the air had brought it to him. But Klávus was not the man he had been. A squall swept him off his feet and flung him headlong into the stream. He swore terribly when he got to his feet, and trembled so much that his teeth chattered. 'You're just a forgotten old wretch,' he told himself. 'You ought never to rise to your feet again. You're no use to anyone – and, as sinful dust, you should be trodden beneath the foot of man.'

But he rose to his feet again and clung to his stick. Once again he let a squall take him, and he was flung against the laths of a storehouse, but they remained unbreached. No, there was nothing more to be done; Klávus went home again empty-handed. 'This is the last time I shall go out in this way,' he said. And he went into one of the little kiln-houses where the villagers dried their half-ripe barley over peat fires at harvest time. Here he fell on his knees and prayed. 'Lord, restore Thy mercy towards me, and grant me my food more easily than hitherto. Let not my enemies rejoice to see me and my family languish before Thy face. Amen.' Then he went home.

The next morning, folk saw Klávus leave the village in his Sunday best. That evening he returned, carrying a sack over his back. People stopped him to admire him. 'Bless me, you're a brisk old fellow, to carry a load like that on your back,' they would say. Where had he been?

He had been to bid people farewell. 'I am finished with life now,' he said. 'I wanted to call on people once more, before I commit myself into the hands of the Lord. But you know how folk are on an occasion like this; they overwhelmed me with gifts, and I don't know – I hadn't the heart to throw them back in their faces!'

Folk laughed. 'That old rogue Klávus! He always manages to get by in one way or another!'

Before long, the wool which Ketil and his wife had brought home was all knitted up. They counted the sweaters back into the sack.

'What do you think we'll get for these?' Ketil asked.

'I don't know, but we'll get something. But we must get in a bit more wool. The nights are so long, we can't just sit down with our arms folded.'

Ketil agreed. 'But the weather is good enough for outdoor work now, so I'd better not spend the daytime spinning.'

'What are you going to do?'

'There's always something to *do*, but the point is, it'll soon be Martinmas now, and we haven't got enough in hand to pay the whale-meat bill. If only I could find something to do that I could get a little *money* for!'

'That's far from easy to find in a village like ours. But another thing is, whether you shouldn't sell off a bit of the meat. If Kálvur leaves us now, we two old folk won't want to eat so much of it.'

No, Ketil would not do that. 'I'll soon be a worn-out old man. I don't expect to be able to get any more, so I can't bring myself to carry food out of my storehouse and hand it over to strangers. If I were young, it would be a different matter altogether.'

'Do what you think's right, but it's just this. I can't see any way out. We're not going to get out of this trouble. And it's always been my great fear, getting into debt.'

Ketil became angry at this, and told her to hold her tongue. 'I can't bear to listen to you any longer. Until the District Sheriff has been here to demand payment, there's no call to give up hope. It may yet be that I'll be able to pay the bill when it comes.' It was late in the evening, but he went and fetched his shoes.

'Are you going out as late as this?'

He made no answer.

'Are you putting on your shoes?' she asked again.

He did not answer a word. So she stopped speaking as well, but she dragged a stool in front of the door, and sat down to knit with her back firmly planted against it.

The anger fell from him, he hung up his shoes again, and his face resumed its customary mildness. Then he squeezed himself down beside her on the stool. She smiled up at him and asked him why he didn't go out.

'You're a sly one, you are,' he laughed, and the two of them sat down in silence.

This was how it had been, the time when Ketil was a young man and had taken to going out drinking with the boys. When he came back a bit merry, and she did not want him to go out again, she used to sit in front of the door. Then he would storm around indoors, until he was weary of it, but it always ended by their both going to bed in the best of good humour. But she had ceased doing anything like this a very long time ago now. So the memories flooded back to him now that she sat that way once again. He turned all sentimental, and patted her affectionately.

The next day they went out with the sweaters and fetched home another sack of wool.

CHAPTER SEVEN

When they got back from the shop, Ketil sat down heavy-hearted on the fireside seat, his elbows on his knees and his beard in his hand.

'You do sit staring so,' said his wife.

'It's worrying about ways and means, that's all. There's nothing to live on any longer, and no way of making a cent.'

'Hang on now, don't give up hope,' said his wife comfortingly. 'Perhaps the Lord will set us on our feet once again.'

'How? No fishing weather, no nothing. I think the Lord Himself must realise how things are here now. I didn't sleep a wink last night.'

'I know that; you were tossing and turning the whole time. But I tell you again what I told you before: sell some of the whale meat, just a bit of it. We've scraped a bit of money together, and the cow will calve in about a week, so we can fatten up the calf. If you got a bit for the meat, maybe we'd be covered.'

Ketil did not dismiss this idea outright. 'Yes, it could well be, if you think it's all right. It was silly of me, perhaps, to set myself against it. But who's going to buy the meat? Everyone on this island's got more than enough.'

'Go to Tórshavn.'

'Me go to Tórshavn? I've not been there in forty years. I'm not going to set foot in Tórshavn.'

'If it's better to be sold up, don't go then,' teased his wife.

'What would I do in Tórshavn, where everything's so fine? And who do I know whom I could ask to buy?'

'You don't need to know anyone. They'll come themselves. Tie up to the quay, set the meat ashore, and wait for them.'

But Ketil was still unwilling. 'I'd only get myself into a mess doing that. And where would I stay? Every time I wanted a bite to eat, I'd have to sit and fumble around with a fork and bring shame on myself.'

'There are plenty of places in Tórshavn that take in guests.'

'Yes, and in return they'd want all the money I made from the meat, and perhaps more on top of that. And what do you do with yourself if you're taken short, with people about all over the place?' No, he wouldn't move an inch towards Tórshavn. Then he went out of the house.

In the evening he came back and told his wife that he had just been to the shop to borrow the dragnet. They would go over to West Bay to set it, for the weather was just right.

'So you won't be going to Tórshavn, then?'

'No, I'm not going to go peddling whale meat through the streets of Tórshavn,' he replied.

'How are you going to get the net to West Bay?'

'I'll ask our eldest son to take it in the big boat.' Then he sat down to sew up woollen shoes. He was much more cheerful now that he had a netting expedition planned, and had got his wife to stop talking about going to Tórshavn. He took a brand from the fire, lit his pipe, and went over to his wife, and enveloped her in smoke. 'Now we'll get so many piltocks, old girl, that we'll sell their livers by the barrelful, you'll see.'

The following afternoon Ketil, with four of his sons and two of his sons-in-law, sailed over to set the net. When they were about to set off, the old man didn't want to go with them. 'I don't mind walking over to West Bay in good weather like this,' he said.

'None of that damn nonsense,' they said, pulling him into the boat and casting off. When the motor had started, Ketil laughed. 'Damn these things! But they're handy to have, all the same.' Even so, he put an oar out, because it always saved a drop or two of petrol.

Kálvur was lying in the front, saying 'Hup!' every time the boat slid down a trough to strike the oncoming wave and fling its water away from the bows. 'Father, there's a big difference between when you row and when the motor rows. There's a much bigger bow wave now,' he told the old man.

They reached West Bay, and put some men ashore with the line, while the rest of them went out again to set the net.

Ketil and Kálvur both went ashore. While they were waiting for the boat to come in again, they walked along the shore northwards. There might always be something lying on the beach that could be put to good use. When they reached the western end, they saw a little old man sitting on a stone with a fishing rod.

'Lord have mercy on us, who is it here as late as this on a mid-winter day?' Ketil went over to him. It was Lias Berint.

He and Ketil were of an age, for they had been confirmed together. Ketil began to laugh. 'Now you've got me baffled. Are you living like an outlaw, up in the hills, in your old age?'

Lias Berint laughed back in return. 'You might well say so, but it's not exactly that. I just thought of getting myself a bit of food this way.'

'Food, did you say? Don't you live with your niece?'

'Yes, to be sure I do, but this is the point. They've applied to have me put on the rates, so I thought I'd set up somewhere on my own. It's so miserable, not owning your own store of food.'

'Somebody must have been fooling you,' remarked Ketil. 'They wouldn't put in a claim on the rates just to feed you. Anyway, you're not altogether lacking in land, are you?'

'No, I've got my ancestral lands, to be sure I have, three guilder of land,* so it's a great disgrace to be made a pauper.'

Ketil agreed with him. 'But look, you can't spend the night out here. Come and help us pull in the net, and then you can come back to the village in our boat. Our home's no palace, but you'll get a roof over your head if you like. There aren't many of us at home now, fortunately.'

'Thank you, thank you,' said Lias Berint happily. 'It's good to have some place where you're welcome. A friend in need is a friend indeed.' They agreed that he should come and live with Ketil, at least until something else turned up.

---

* The Faroese guilder – gyllin – is a highly variable unit, but three guilder would be about a quarter of an acre of cultivated infield, and sufficient moorland grazing for four sheep.

Then they went back to the others. 'What old bit of wreckage has Father found this time?' they joked.

Soon it darkened. There was some moonshine, but through an overcast sky. It was calm. The waves lapped on the shore, and the eider-ducks lay chattering in the seaweed.

The net was set, and the dragline rowed back to land. Then they all pulled it in. Ketil and Lias Berint sat in the back, coiling up the rope. 'An old man does his work best when he's on his backside,' they agreed. 'Let the younger fellows do the hauling.'

So they sat down, puffing at their pipes and joking. Lias Berint had lost all his teeth, but he had wound a rag round his pipestem, so it smoked quite well. He shivered, and wrapped his jacket close around himself. He had pulled up his stockings over his trouser legs, because it kept him warmer that way. The new age had come to Lias Berint from above – he had a cloth cap on his head. But to diminish its foreign appearance he had pulled the peak off. Bits of sacking and newspaper were hanging from the opening. 'But to hell with that,' thought Lias Berint. 'I'm amongst my own countrymen, aren't I?'

'You never got married, did you?' Ketil teased his friend.

No, he didn't know how it was, but he'd never had good luck with womenfolk that way. 'And blast them, they're so quicktempered, I've never been very eager to get too close with them. No, you have to handle them like cats, my friend – stroke them when they're friendly, but the moment they begin to spit, put a boot into their backsides.' And Lias Berint laughed and scratched his head.

The net came to the shore. The young men waded out to

turn the corners and pull the net together. 'Don't you old fellows get yourselves wet. We can manage it,' they said.

But the old men were not to be reasoned with. They stood right by the water's edge, watching. When they saw that the net was seething with fish, they both jumped forward. 'Ah, we're truly blessed in this catch,' they cried.

'Hell and damnation, keep off the line!' shouted one of the young men.

'Now then, guard your tongue,' Lias Berint warned him. 'Don't anger God when the catch has not yet been brought to land.'

The old men joined in the work of ladling out the fish with baskets. They worked passionately. The young men were staggered; they had never seen such triumph over a catch – after all, it was only a few piltocks.

There was just about a boatful in the net.

They set the net again. While the boat was away, the ones who stayed on the shore built a stone enclosure for the fish. The young men wanted to build another, ready for the next catch, but the old ones would not agree to this. 'You shouldn't lay stones around fish that are still swimming in the sea. The Lord doesn't approve of presumption of that sort.'

But the young men told them to stow that sort of talk, and they laid stones as they pleased.

While they were sitting and waiting for the boat, Kálvur went to his father and complained of the cold. 'We'd be better off if we went right home, so I could get into dry clothes,' he said.

'To hell with that,' said Ketil angrily. 'You shouldn't always

107

be so ready to give up. The weather's like Midsummer Night, so we must try to catch a lot of piltocks.'

'Young flesh feels the cold more,' said Lias Berint, 'but maybe there's a cure for it.' He called Kálvur over to him. They walked up the hill together. 'Now, I'll pull up some withered grass from a dry slope, and stuff it into your breeches. Then you'll keep a lot warmer.'

Kálvur did not really care for the idea, however, thinking it was a bit odd to walk around with that stuff in your breeches. He blushed and pushed his forefinger into his mouth; but he could not bring himself to refuse, because it was a stranger who was pushing in the grass. It wasn't warm either, for the grass was damp. They rejoined the others, and sat down.

Then the boat came back, and all of them went to haul the line except Kálvur, who remained sitting there. Ketil called out to him and asked if he wasn't going to help the others, but he got no reply. So he went over to him. 'What's the matter?' he said. Kálvur was sitting there crying.

'Listen, lad, what's up? Are you sick?'

'No, but I'm so afraid,' sniffed Kálvur.

'You're a real coward. Just put yourself into God's keeping, and don't make a fuss.'

'Yes, but I've found five sand hoppers or something of that sort alive in my breeches, and there are ever so many more, and they're scratching me everywhere,' wept Kálvur.

'Oh, be quiet with you. Whoever heard of a fisherman crying over sand hoppers?' Ketil left him, fuming.

But soon, Kálvur was so plagued by the sand hoppers that he had to take off his trousers and turn them out.

That time, they hauled another boatload of fish in with their net.

Some of the men now began to argue that it would be best to send back to the village for more boats, but the old men disagreed. 'If you get a great crowd of folk around, each man's share of fish will be next to nothing.' So they agreed to continue fishing for a bit more of the night, and then go home, leaving the catch lying on the beach.

They drew the net three times more, and caught many more fish. Then it was so late that the men were tired, and glad to return home.

But the old men would not accompany them. 'We're not going to leave the catch unguarded,' they said.

'Who do you think's going to come out to West Bay to steal piltocks?' the young men asked.

'It would be all the same, whether it was beasts out of the sea, or birds from the air.'

The boat left them.

The old men walked up to a sheep shelter near the beach, and kindled a fire. 'Now we can have a really fine meal of piltocks,' they said. They had taken a pan from the boat to cook them in.

While the water was heating up, they took off their shoes, hung their stockings up to dry, and toasted their feet on the hearthstones. Then they leaned right back against the wall of the shelter, chuckled to one another, and lit up their pipes. 'The sea – it's a real blessing to us, the way it gives us catch after catch. One day you've not got a mouthful left, the next day your storehouse is overflowing.' They talked on in this fashion.

Round about them was the stillness of the night. The moon had set, and they listened to the sound of the streams and the shore.

When the piltocks were boiled, they took them off the fire, and ate till they were nearly bursting.

Then Lias Berint said, 'Many's the time we've felt the pinch, but taking it all around, would you and I want to change places with anyone else?'

'No,' said Ketil, 'it's good as it is. I'm an old man now, with one foot in the grave, but this I can say, we've never gone short of food in our house, God be praised, though it's often looked pretty bleak, I must admit.'

'I can say the same,' answered Lias Berint. 'I've never had my own home. I've always lodged with other folk, ever since I was a boy. But I've always had a roof over my head, and never have I gone hungry.'

'Yes, and if we can't be content with that,' said Ketil, 'what more can a poor man ask for? That's what I'm always telling the youngsters.' He stretched out his legs and belched. 'I'm getting sleepy now I'm full,' he continued. 'Perhaps we'd better lie down and have a bit of a nap.'

'It's a help,' answered Lias Berint, 'if we gather up withered grass and put it down for us to lie on.'

So the two old men tottered out barefoot into the night. Above them was the black basalt cliff shutting off the southern sky. The bountiful sea now stretched out peacefully the other side of them.

A sheep suddenly wandered in from its sheltering-place, stared at them with green eyes, and disappeared. 'Sirra-sirra-sirra,' they called into the dark to it. 'Come on, we won't harm you.'

'Withered grass,' said Lias Berint, 'it's a grand thing, useful in all sorts of ways. When God sends a blessing on the withered grass, the farmer lives well, but if it gets snowed under too much, then he's like you and me – he must seek his food from the sea.'

They heard the faint roar of breakers on the distant rocks. 'Cormorant Skerries are noisy tonight,' said Ketil. 'They're grimmer, though, when a north-easter's blowing.'

They came nearer to the stream now, and heard that still louder. He was a friendly fellow, lying and chattering here in the outfield pasture. The two men had at times seen it both larger and smaller than it was tonight, so they talked about that. 'But it's always here. I never remember it to have been completely dried up, even in the worst of droughts,' they said.

Each of them gathered up his armful of grass, and spread it out on the floor of the sheep shelter. They laid plenty of peat on the fire, and then lay down to sleep.

At daybreak they awoke in a cold sweat ... they heard men's voices. They leapt to their feet, crying, 'Damn and blast them, they're stealing our fish.'

They were Lias Berint's fellow villagers, who had been searching for him all night. 'Oh, you old devil, you're here are you? What do you mean by slinking off like this and getting folk into a panic searching for you?'

Lias Berint thought it was a shame for them, but deemed it wisest to be a bit sharp with them, or they might start begging for some fish. So he said, 'I reckon to make up my own mind where I go. I'm a free man – and I didn't ask anyone to come out looking for me. You ought to have stayed at home.'

So the search party went off.

The old men got the fire going and put the pot on again. Now there was no time to sleep any more, as they had to look after the catch. 'For when the daylight comes, creation begins to stir again. Ah, it's a grand life, looking after the catch!'

Later in the day they were able to go home.

The young men had carried word to the village about what Ketil had found on the beach this time.

'Just wait and see,' the people said. 'Why do you think Ketil's bringing him home? Only to wheedle his land out of him. Anything that turns up, that man's got his claws right into it. Why else should he want to go over to West Bay with the dragnet? Hasn't he raked together enough yet? No, what I say is, he's on to the scent of something, the old devil.'

And folk crowded to the windows to gaze, when Ketil and Lias Berint came back. Children stood right in the middle of the lane gaping at them. Some even ran along behind them shouting, 'Beachcomber, beachcomber!'

Ketil's wife received them kindly, with hot coffee and dry clothes. A peat fire was roaring away in the hearth. 'God looks down in mercy on the poor man,' she thought about Lias Berint.

'Now, you must have some coffee first,' she said. 'When you've changed into dry things, you can have a meal. Then you can go to bed.'

The old men were very grateful for the coffee and the meal, but they would not go to bed. When they were warm and well fed, they began to sharpen their filleting knives. 'We must think about the catch before we think about sleep,' they said.

As long as there was any daylight, they went over to fetch home piltocks and share them out. The share belonging to

Ketil's household they took to his hayhouse and flung them down there. From there, they took them into his living room to gut them.

But Kálvur wanted to give up. 'I'm so tired, I can't do any more. You'll have to do the gutting yourselves.'

'That's no good,' snapped Ketil. 'Even if you are tired, you'll still come and help us. Who do you suppose isn't tired? When I was your age, I was never asked whether I was tired or not. I had to carry on working till it was finished, so I didn't bring shame on myself, and so that the job was done.' Ketil gave him a knife, and he had to help with the gutting.

Ketil's wife lit the lamp and drove the hens into the byre, for it was no good having them sitting on the beams and dropping anything this evening. Then she hitched up her petticoat, took up a knife, and began to help as well. 'I can give you a hand until it's time to get supper,' she said.

Then the pastor came in and asked them to sell him some fish. 'Certainly,' they said, 'how many do you want? About thirty? Oh, no, you're not going to pay anything. You were so kind as to lend us your horse the other day.'

'Yes, but that was the very least I could do,' said the pastor, who laid a krone on the end of the bench as he left.

The pastor had hardly gone when Klávus arrived. He stretched out over the heap of fish on the bench and lay on his side. 'Praised be God that you have made such a fine catch! God is good, and gives even the unrepentant sinner his daily bread.'

'How are you getting on now, Klávus?' asked Ketil. 'Are you strong and fit once again? I hear you're not often with us here in the village these days, but that you travel all around the place.'

Yes, Klávus could not grumble. He had been blessed with many small mercies lately. And you could certainly see that he'd had enough to eat lately, for he had begun to fill his jacket out, and his wife was no longer gaunt, but had a paunch on her and new teeth.

'There's another thing about piltocks,' said Klávus. 'The only men who can catch them are those who are specially favoured by God. The poor sickly wretch can only rejoice that these blessings shower down on others. But in the day when the stars fall from heaven, the fountains of the deep are broken up, and the waters spread over the face of the earth – then shall the name of him who has aided the helpless wretch in his time of need be written in the Book of Life.'

Ketil got up and gave him some fish.

'Thank you, thank you,' said Klávus. 'God sees into the heart of man, and will reward even this small gift, when the seventh seal is broken.' Then he went.

But Lias Berint shouted after him, 'Don't leave us so soon! Hang on a bit. You're ever such a clever priest – your words become fish, straight away.'

But Klávus would not stay. He slipped out of the door.

'So you see how to do it,' laughed Lias Berint. 'If we two had been as clever as that, we'd be fat and sleek.'

But Ketil did not think it was clever. 'I would rather die than go around begging,' he said.

Then a heavy downpour began. They could hear the rain thundering on the roof, and great black drops began to fall down inside.

'Damn me if it isn't leaking,' grumbled Ketil. He took his hat and wiped the sooty water off his neck with it. 'My roof was ripped up in that storm not long ago. Otherwise it would have been dry enough here.'

'Never mind that,' replied Lias Berint, scratching between his shoulder blades. 'Everyone suffers from leaks and fleas, as the saying goes. But my old grandfather used to say, "Lice are shameful, but even a gentleman can have fleas in his house".'

Kálvur burst out laughing. The others asked him why. He replied that he thought it was so funny to hear the people of the house talk about fleas.

Ketil's wife laid down her knife, went over to the fish, and started rooting around among them.

'What are you scratching around like a dog for?' asked Ketil.

'I thought I'd cook you some stuffed piltocks for supper, so I wanted to find some of the bigger ones,' she replied.

It was as though Lias Berint had taken wing. 'Jesus bless us, stuffed piltocks! I've been living with a wealthy sloop skipper for eleven years, but never have I as much as tasted stuffed piltocks.' And the old man's mouth watered so much that he had to swallow hard.

'I can believe that,' said Ketil's wife, 'but you've had finer food, the sort people eat who live from the shops.'

'I don't know how they live,' gasped Lias Berint, 'but it doesn't suit me. Food's not worth eating, the way they slop everything together on one plate. You can't even have a chunk of whale meat unless it's cut up, or messed around in a frying-pan. And then that damned sauce – God forgive my words – which you can never escape. You can't take hold of a piece for fear of scalding yourself. And I've always hated forks.'

Then Kálvur said, 'If it had been me, I would have made myself a little pair of tongs to take the pieces up with.'

'Hold your tongue,' snapped Ketil, 'don't sit around all the time joining in the talk, when old folk are speaking. You ought to be going out and taking people some fish. It's the old custom to take a cooking around to every house in the neighbourhood when you fetch home a catch.'

But no, Kálvur would not dare to. It was so dark, and the stream had burst its banks. 'Perhaps there'll be lightning,' he said.

'Nonsense. Put on an oilskin. The lightning won't eat you.' Kálvur had to go.

'Thank you,' said the womenfolk, when Kálvur arrived with the fish. 'Thank your mother very much.' The men stretched out enviously on their fireside seats and said nothing.

When Kálvur came to the door of Klávus's house, he had an impulse to go in and do some courting, but he didn't dare to, because his girl had caught the itch, and Klávus had tarred her for it. So he went home.

Ketil sent him off again. 'Go over to Klávus and borrow us a few planks. We can't sit here under these leaks, it isn't comfortable.'

But Klávus would not lend them any, and said he didn't have any.

'Shame on the fellow who won't help out,' said Ketil angrily. 'But we'll manage yet.' Then they took three doors off their hinges and set them up across the beams. They put all the pots and pans that were in the house on top to catch the drips, and then moved around until they each found a dry place to sit in.

Then six grandchildren came blustering in.

'What are you out in this bad weather for?' asked Ketil. 'Have you come for some fish?'

'No, we've got so much ourselves, but Father's asking you and the visitor to come over.'

'Yes, we'll come over, as soon as we've had a bit of supper. Does he want anything in particular?'

They didn't know.

Supper was ready. The old woman took the pot off the fire, cleared a space among the heap of fish for it, and bade them help themselves.

Ketil took a fragment of washing soap and went out to the stream to wash the slime and scales off his hands, but Lias Berint simply wiped his hands on the grass of the roof. 'There's nothing dirty about that stuff,' he said. Then they sat down in the same places where they had been gutting fish, to have their supper.

Kálvur took his share on the pot lid. 'It's so tiring to sit where you can't lean back,' he said. So he squeezed himself into the corner at the end of the bench, and ate till he fell asleep.

Before they went over to the eldest son's, they carried the rest of the fish in from the hayhouse into the living room. Now there was not a single bare patch on the floor. They thought they had done pretty well, for the heap that was left over was smaller than they had expected.

When they got over there, the eldest son was sitting at the kitchen table, all clean and neat. His wife was just washing herself.

'Well then,' they said, 'have you finished gutting?'

Yes, everything was now stowed away.

The old men gasped and goggled. Already finished with the gutting? But they said nothing.

'No, it wasn't anything I wanted,' said the eldest son. 'It was just for company's sake I asked you over. I thought you might like a drop of spirits, now you're through with your gutting.' He pulled out a flask, fetched a glass, and passed them over. 'I'm not going to pour out for you – just take as much as you want to.'

'Thanks, that's good of you.' They drank the glass out, but said that was quite enough. Now they must go.

'Are you in such a hurry?' asked the eldest son. 'Haven't you finished gutting?'

No, they hadn't finished.

'Well then, I'll drop in and see you later on.'

When they got outside, they did not say a word. They just walked on, reflecting how they were no match for the young folk in gutting fish. When they passed Klávus's storehouse, there was a lamp burning inside, and through the laths they could see that Klávus was there splitting up fish. 'What I gave him stretches out farther than you'd expect,' said Ketil.

'He's doubtless had fish from others than us.'

'No, he's not had any from other people. He's stolen the rest from us. But let him keep what he wants. He's a miserable creature, and there's nothing you can do about it.'

When they got home, Ketil's wife was looking pleased. 'It's good you came back. Did they want you to help with their gutting?' Neither of them answered. They pushed the heap of offal to one side and began gutting again.

Ketil's wife began to laugh. 'Whatever happened to you over there, to make you so tongue-tied? Has our fine daughter-in-law shown you the door? Perhaps she thought you were too dirty to tread on her carpets? It's a pity you didn't go over in your Sunday best. She'd have done better to have helped her husband to get the fish in order. It's a real shame for folk to have a catch of fish in their houses when they don't bother to look after it. But it's the sure sign of the incompetent to let your own goods go to rack and ruin, and run to others when you get into difficulties.'

Then Ketil ripped a fish right in half, and gave his wife a sharp look. 'Why are you bitching about your daughter-in-law? Do you know whether she has, or hasn't done anything with the fish?'

'Didn't you say she hadn't touched them?'

'No, I didn't say that.'

'Didn't you say as well, that she showed you the door?'

'No, I didn't say that either.'

'All right then, why are you sitting there dumb? Have you lost your voice?'

'Your daughter-in-law *did* help her husband with the gutting,' said Ketil. 'She was just washing herself afterwards. She was friendly, and did not show us the door. They have finished *their* gutting.'

'It's a bit late to tell me now,' said the old woman sharply. 'Why didn't you tell me that right away, instead of letting me stand here criticising them when they don't deserve it? They've finished gutting already? Have you been bungling the job then – three men at it and still half to do?'

Lias Berint sat muttering into his beard. 'Now, has anyone ever seen anything like these womenfolk? And this old harridan of Ketil's, she's just like the rest of them, I can see that,' he said to himself.

Then the eldest son came in. He stepped back into the doorway. 'Good God!' he said, 'what a pigsty you've got the place into here!'

'Pigsty? What do you mean?' asked the old woman. 'We have to be thankful to God that food is coming into the house even if it does make a mess.' She stood by the fire kneading dough.

'Be thankful to God, yes,' mimicked the son; 'sit in filth and thank God, that's just like you. Damn me if the right thing to do wouldn't be to burn down the whole muck heap about your ears.' He was almost angry, and went out.

Shortly afterwards he came back with two brothers. All were in oilskins. They fetched down a couple of tubs from the loft. First they stowed away the gutted fish, and after that they gathered up the offal and got it out of the house.

The old folk who had been sitting and gutting were pushed to one side, and retired, pale and indignant, muttering to themselves, but not saying a word aloud. And the young folk were not especially tactful in the way they spoke. The middlemost son said to Lias Berint, when he moved away from the heap, 'Now, old chap, try and climb up out of the shit. Make some progress, or at least let our generation do it.' To Ketil he said, 'You come to anchor by the fireplace, Father, and lift your feet high enough for me to get the muck away from under you.'

The old men gnashed their teeth so much that their beards danced a tattoo on their shirts, but they said not a word.

The sons put all the fish that still remained to be gutted into a box in the yard, cleaned the earth floor of the living room as well as they could, spread an old sail on the floor, brought in a tub of fish at a time, and settled down to gut them.

The eldest son laughed up at the old men. 'Now, we've cleared that muck heap away. Now make a good fire up, to dry out the house after the tidal wave that's been through here.'

Later, they asked for hot water to make themselves some punch. They drank it from great beakers, and ate sugar with it. 'You old fellows,' they said, 'come and get a good swig of this to wash the fish scales out of you, and then turn in. There's nothing for tired old fellows to gape at.'

No, they wouldn't drink anything.

'Don't come out with the sulks now. Have we got to be snubbed in return for lending you a hand?'

Then Lias Berint cleared his throat and gave a little chuckle. 'Perhaps I might have a drop,' he said.

Ketil also gave in and drank a fair amount.

'No need to hold yourselves back,' joked the young men, 'you're very welcome to it. It's not everyone of your age who manages as well as you two. But drop the old men's talk of the world being out of joint, and young people not being able to do anything.'

'Maybe it's we who are out of joint,' said the old men, as they went stiff and weary to bed.

The next day, Ketil went happily to the shop to sell the fish livers.

CHAPTER EIGHT

One morning the doctor came to the village in hot haste. The womenfolk crowded to the windows, but much to their vexation, they couldn't make out what his errand might be. An hour passed before they learned anything; but then Tummas came through the lane with the news.

'It's the pastor's wife who sent for him. One of her children is ill.'

'You don't know what's wrong?' asked the womenfolk.

No, Tummas didn't know. 'But of course, it could be measles, you know; they've got measles in the southern islands.' Then he stuck his hands into his trouser pockets, shrugged his shoulders, and went on.

It was a sorrowful morning in Ketil's house. No one had the strength to utter a word. Ketil's wife slammed the door shut. 'Nobody's going to put a foot over my threshold, you'd better get that clear,' she said. 'We're going to keep ourselves free of infection. There's not been measles in this village for fifty years. The place will be laid waste.'

Ketil looked down at his feet and folded his hands. 'No

good will come of trying to keep apart, to my way of thinking,' he said. 'If any of our neighbours' households found themselves helpless, they'd have to be given a hand, as long as anyone was on his feet.'

Lias Berint bent forward as he sat, took off his cap and scratched his head. 'Now I'll soon be a pauper after all – living here among strangers, and dying without having the title deeds of my ancestral lands by me, and maybe having borrowed planks to my coffin and bringing myself to shame.'

Kálvur sat with his head on his breast, crying. Once he looked up and asked his father whether there was much sweating when folk died of measles. He was afraid the doctor might go from house to house sticking his instruments into people's backsides. It was so embarrassing showing your private parts to strangers.

The old woman was the first to recover heart. 'Well now, it's no good sitting here moping. We must at all events have the place so neat and tidy here that we're not put to shame if the doctor should have to pay us a call. Only it's a great nuisance washing the place out, when the roof leaks so badly that the sooty water drips all over the place. Ketil, couldn't you get the roof watertight straight away?'

'I'd very gladly have done that already,' replied Ketil, 'if I'd had the necessary materials. We can't afford to buy birch bark yet, before we've paid off the bill for the whale meat. And there's not a straw in the village. One or the other we shall need to hold the turf in place.'

'Well, then, go south to the next village,' said Lias Berint. 'You're bound to get all you want there. I've got a thing or two to do there as well, so I could go in the boat with you, if I wouldn't be in your way.'

'That's a good idea of yours, but the day's half over now, so we can't do anything before tomorrow,' said Ketil.

Before sunrise the following morning, Ketil, Kálvur and Lias Berint set off in the old boat. The old men's arms creaked as they started rowing, and they wrinkled their brows with the pain of rheumatism. But it was nothing to make a fuss about – when old age comes on, you expect to have rheumatism. An old man has to be thankful if he can still get out of bed and put on his own clothes. There are plenty who are not as brisk as that.

The weather was good. They rowed lightly, with a following current, and had the sail up. The shore they were rowing along was black from the night's rain; a few crows flew up cawing from the boulders by the shore, and a sheep got up out of one of the stone shelters and stretched itself. The old men looked up at the sky in silence. 'The sky looks a bit murky. You can't be sure how long the weather's going to stay fine. Maybe it'll hold as long as there's light,' they thought. But they said nothing. A youngster was in the boat, and it was not worth making him nervous.

The boat glided gently southward, lying deep in the water, rather like a purblind sea beast fumbling its way forward. There were patches in her sides, the tar shone thick on her keel, and every plank bore witness to age and wear. But when the breeze freshened a little, and Ketil went back into the stern to steer, you could see how pleased he was with himself. He sat there in the stern, conscious that the boat was his own, whatever it might look like. He thought she sailed quite well. 'The young fellows can laugh at my boat if they like,' he said, 'but let me tell you, she's tight and seaworthy, and that's all you can ask of any boat. Theirs are perhaps prettier, but what's the use of being prettier when they belong to someone else, and for the most part are just for show? Let them fetch as many loads home as this old boat of mine has done, and then their boats won't look so bright and glossy.'

Lias Berint saw a piece of timber in the water, and asked Ketil to steer over to it. It was about as big as a boat stock, but Lias Berint took it in, saying that there was always a use for a piece of wood if you were going to build a house. It would do for a cross-strut.

'Are you going to venture on building at your age?' asked Ketil.

'I've been thinking of doing so for forty years, in Jesus's name. Just as the old proverb has it, "Nothing venture, nothing win". I should have had a lot of timber gathered together by now, but the pieces I stowed away in the earlier years are so rotten that they won't be much use when I come to need them. But be that as it may, I'm not going to wait any longer. I may as well begin the foundations tomorrow as any other day.'

Kálvur sat thinking about meals and measles. He rested his oar, and asked his father for something to eat.

'You're a fine sort of man,' said Ketil, 'wanting to eat already. You know the food chest isn't opened until the return journey.'

'It's all the same,' replied Kálvur. 'Nobody knows when the measles are going to come, and there'll be no eating then, I shouldn't think.'

As they approached the village, they saw about thirty

young men standing on the quay with their hands in their pockets, staring at the mail boat, which was churning in behind them. When they saw Ketil's old boat, they laughed, swore, and crowded around it. They had never seen a boat like that before.

Ketil's party climbed ashore and tied up their boat. Ketil asked a young man standing there whether he knew of anyone who had some straw.

'Straw?' repeated the young man, dragging at his cigarette. 'Sorry, I don't know anything about any straw.' And he turned on his heel and was gone.

In the village, they asked their way until they came to a farmer, who gave them some straw – he was so glad they hadn't come to demand an allotment from his land, that he overwhelmed them with straw, so that Ketil had to say, 'Hold on, hold on, our boat won't carry any more.'

Lias Berint said to Ketil, 'I'll just drop in and see my niece while you're carrying the straw down. Don't go without me.'

He had a fair way to go through the fields. Some way from the houses he sat down for a few minutes to think out what he ought to do. Should he come like an angel, or like a thunderstorm? He didn't know. 'If only I had my temper up, I'd cope with the wretched creatures a bit better,' he thought. He pulled at his beard to try and rouse himself to fury, but the anger was not genuine. So it would be better to approach them calmly. He took a stump of chalk and smeared his beard and his hair. 'They shall see how grey I've turned since I left them,' he thought. As he neared the houses, he tried to look miserable, and put on a limp.

The only one at home was his niece. 'Good day,' said Lias Berint in a mild voice.

'Good day,' answered his niece without looking up. She had her breast hanging out over a baby, which was lying there sucking and clutching at her arm.

'There were just a few things I had ...'

'They're right where you left them.'

He went upstairs to his old room, and took out a little red chest from under the bed. Here he kept his title deeds and his Sunday clothes. He took the chest under one arm and went downstairs again.

'Good-bye,' he forced himself to say as he reached the door.

'Good-bye,' answered his niece, hanging out her other breast for the baby.

Lias Berint stopped, cursing inwardly. 'Damn her, she doesn't as much as look up at me and swear.' But she did not look up. So he went, shutting the door behind him, quietly and patiently. But a little further on, in the fields, he suddenly felt furious. He put down the chest, ran back to the house, and flung the door open. 'Shame on you, niece,' he cried, 'for having the heart to treat me in this way! Look at me, and you'll see how grey I've turned, since I had to leave.' And he pointed to his whitened beard.

'May God forgive you,' she replied. 'We have not pushed you out. You do us an injustice to say any such thing.'

'No, maybe you didn't push me out, but you pushed me on to the rates.'

'No, all we did was to apply for your old-age pension.'

'So I hear, so I hear, and shame on you for doing so. I was

all right for you as long as I was bringing something in to the house, but now I'm an old man, and more or less past work, you push me on to the rates.' He slammed the door behind him and went. And he was so angry, he forgot which leg he was supposed to be lame in. 'But damn it,' he muttered, 'why the devil should I limp for an old harridan like that?' He snorted, until his beard spread out like whiskers on each side of his cheeks. To take a short cut, he went straight across the field. Then he tripped over a tussock and for some time lay there fuming. But now he began to feel afraid. He sat quietly in the grass, crossed himself, and recited the Lord's Prayer. Then he went on again.

He met several of the old men, who came out to talk with him.

'You left the village and deserted us,' they said. Apart from that, it was just the usual they talked about: rheumatism, the weather, and the boat fishing.

Sertus came along and wanted to gossip. He wore a black kerchief round his neck and a linen cloth round his jaw, and his sidewhiskers stood up so high that his hat looked as though it was perched on a nest.

'Do you always go wrapped up?' asked Lias Berint.

'Oh, don't talk about it – I'm no good for anything. These wraps are nothing in particular, just for a gumboil, but there are other things which are a lot worse. You remember the time I broke my bones in five places, when we were in a boat together – once in each shoulder, and in three places in the left thigh? Now I've got a swelling in the throat that I have to take medicine for, and a pain in the loins that I have to massage, so beyond all question I'm the most broken-down old fellow in the village. Lofty Heindrikkur goes around saying that he's worse, they tell me. But what I say is, let him show you where he's sick, if he can. What's wrong with me anybody can look at.' And he showed him the swelling in his throat, and took hold of his breeches and was going to pull them down to show his thigh, but Lias Berint told him he had to hurry. 'For it's getting late. Why don't you go and see the doctor?'

'See the doctor!' snapped Sertus. 'I've seen the doctor often enough. But I don't know, doctors nowadays are not a patch on what they used to be. That's what I always say, although folk laugh at me for it. It's a sure fact that the doses they give you nowadays are smaller than the ones the old doctors used to give you.'

But Lias Berint had to go. 'Good-bye, Sertus,' he said. 'Good-bye, old friend, good-bye, don't let me hold you up. No, I don't trust these doctors nowadays. It's better to rely on a man like Klávus. They tell me he's left the Church of Denmark and joined a sect. But it's all the same to me, he's strong in the faith, for if you get him to lay his hands on you, it helps a good deal.'

Lias Berint ran to escape from the fellow, but Sertus followed him as well as he could.

When Lias Berint came to the quay, Ketil and Kálvur had loaded the straw into the boat, and were lying there waiting. The old man came on board, buried his chest under the straw, and sat down.

They pulled away from the land. A stack of straw was at each end of the boat, and between the thwarts they had loaded the boat up to the gunwales. The weather was still calm, but the sky was more threatening than ever. 'It could hold till nightfall,' the old men ruminated.

When they had gone some distance, they opened the food chest, cut themselves a few pieces, and ate them as they rowed.

'I've never carried a fuller load of straw in this boat,' said Ketil. 'It'll be easy to stop the leaks in the roof now.'

'Will you use all this straw?' asked Lias Berint.

'I don't know. But no, I couldn't! There's such a quantity of it.'

'It was just that if you should have a truss or two over, perhaps you could let me have it. Even if I don't build straight away, I can store it up.'

Ketil agreed to do this.

Kálvur sat sucking sugar candy, and rowed eagerly. He was looking forward to all the rye bread he would eat when they held their thatching party. He asked his father how many men he would invite to share the work.

'None,' replied the old man.

Then Kálvur began to sulk, because there wouldn't be a party. He inwardly swore that he would stop putting any weight into his rowing. 'Damn me if I'm going to sweat myself if there isn't a square meal to look forward to,' he thought.

While they were passing the deserted ferry landing at Fútaklettur, a rainstorm swept down from the northwest, and blotted out the sound ahead of them. When they were off Oyragjógv, they ran into the weather. The first squall turned their boat round, and the storm now sprang up so fast that they could never get their bow back into the wind. They were driven broadside on towards the shore, struck a boulder, heeled over, and the straw slipped into the water. All three of them jumped out and flung the straw onto the shore, before it blew away.

But while they were engaged in doing this, Lias Berint let out a heart-rending cry for help. His chest with his title deeds and his Sunday clothes was drifting away, blown southward down the sound. All three of them hurried along the rocky coast, expecting it to be blown ashore again somewhere. Lias Berint was in front. Bareheaded, and with stockings hanging down, he ran as if his life depended on it, shouting and invoking God. 'Jesus, Jesus, save my precious chest, save my ancestral lands and my Sunday clothes, my hope of salvation!' He ran on as fast as he could go, with the others behind him. The salt water flung itself off them, their beards flapped in the wind, and they stared beseechingly at the chest, making one vow after another for its safe return. When all was of no avail, tears filled their eyes, and they clenched their fists, threatening the chest, frantically appealing to God, losing all control of themselves – for if God did intend to restore the chest to Lias, He had not a moment to lose.

Lias Berint stood on the edge of a small basalt cliff. He now realised that the chest was irretrievably lost, and he kneeled on a rock to pray, and beseech God for its return. But the stone was a loose one, and he rolled with it, over the edge of the cliff.

'Are you hurt?' shouted Ketil to him. Lias Berint did not answer, but lay there motionless. Ketil climbed down and took him up, but he was dead. The fall had been only a short one, but his skull was fractured. For a few moments, Ketil stood quietly over him, his hands buried in his face. Then he went silently back to his son, who sat waiting for him on the clifftop.

'Has Lias Berint hurt himself, Father?' Kálvur asked.

'Lias Berint has passed into the Lord's keeping,' Ketil replied.

They unloaded the stranded boat and pulled it ashore. They carried the straw into a boathouse, the only building on this desolate shore, maintained by the men of Sandavágur, four miles away over the mountains, on the other side of the island.

As dusk fell, the wind dropped a little and the sky began to clear.

Ketil took the rope out of the boat. 'We won't get the body up unless we use rope,' he said.

'Father, I'd be scared to come and help,' said Kálvur.

'Don't be silly, lad, I can't pull him up by myself, and he can't be left out there, at the mercy of the waves of the sea and the birds of the air.' So they went together, though Kálvur trembled like a leaf, and his legs would scarcely carry him. He fell down time after time.

The old man climbed down with one end of the rope and fastened it around Lias Berint. 'Haul away,' he called up to his son.

'I'm scared to, Father.'

'Oh, don't talk nonsense, there's nothing to be afraid of. I'll hold him from below.'

So Kálvur hauled away, but he placed himself a long way back from the edge of the cliff, and shut his eyes. Ketil pushed from below, and they got him up on the ledge. Kálvur, his eyes shut, pulled until he had the corpse actually in his arms. Then he let out a piercing shriek and was about to run up the hillside. But when he saw how harmless Lias Berint seemed, he recovered heart, and asked his father when the funeral would be – he was rather fond of sago soup. The old man did not answer this, but told Kálvur to take hold under the dead man's knees. Then they carried him back along the coast, and laid him in the stern of a boat that was lying in the boathouse.

Then Kálvur began to complain of the cold.

'We could walk home,' said Ketil, 'but it's not right to leave a dead body unaccompanied in this deserted place, so we shall have to stay here for the night.'

Kálvur was appalled by this. 'Are we going to spend the whole of the night here in the pitch dark, wet through and without a fire?' he said.

'I can't help that. We've come here, and here we've got to stay. Give thanks to God that we've reached land at all.'

So they made themselves a comfortable place in the bow of the boat, with straw under them and over them, and they lay down peacefully. They set the food chest in front of them. There was still a bit left in it, but they had come through so much that they had no appetite, and besides, they were so cold they thought it best to burrow into the straw before they froze.

The boathouse stood on the shore at the mouth of a gully. There were black cliffs on both sides of them, a waterfall behind, and the breakers at their feet. Darkness was just falling.

Kálvur lay tense and listening. Every time he heard a sound, he asked his father what it was. The old man bade him be easy. 'It was a puff of wind, blowing under the roof, or a mouse perhaps. Commit yourself into God's hands, and lie down and sleep. Nothing can work us any evil. We are treading our lawful paths and have nothing to be afraid of.'

A little afterwards, Kálvur asked him, 'Have they been for the soul of Lias Berint?'

'Who?'

'The angels.'

'Oh yes, as soon as the spirit left the body, they carried it away.'

'Wouldn't he feel awkward when he got to Heaven, where everything is so fine and there are so many strangers?'

'There is nothing to feel awkward about where nobody makes fun of you.'

'Did it hurt Lias Berint when he died?'

'No, he couldn't have known a thing.'

Kálvur was silent for a time. Then he said, 'Then I think I would have liked to be in Lias Berint's place.'

'Why do you say that?'

'Because then nobody would make fun of me any more.'

'Don't take it to heart, lad, when people make fun of you. They like you well enough all the same – it's just a bit of a joke.'

'I don't think they do like me, because whenever I'm going to say something, they tell me to shut up because I'm a half-wit. Father, is it true I'm a half-wit?'

'You're not a half-wit. As long as you trust in the Lord, you're wise enough.'

Then Kálvur fell asleep, while Ketil lay awake, watching over his comrade in the stern. He took a wet box of matches out of his jacket pocket and laid them against his bare chest. 'Maybe they'll dry out enough by morning to be usable,' he thought.

When the storm broke, Ketil's wife became very worried. She walked backwards and forwards, praying Jesus to have mercy on them. Now they could not get back to the village. Twilight came, and still no boat. Then she went outside, and got a child to go and ask her eldest son to come over.

As darkness was beginning to fall, he came.

'I'm rather worried about the boat. It's not come back, and now there's this bad weather, and night's come on,' she said.

'Just like him, to wander off and get into difficulties,' said her son. 'I thought at the time, he wouldn't come back unless the calm weather held. Neither his boat nor his crew are fit for a long journey. Why didn't he tell me he was going off? I don't know what's the matter with you two. It's almost as if you thought we weren't good enough for you to ask us to do you a favour.'

He said he would go to the phone. Perhaps they had not left the other village.

Soon afterwards, Klávus looked in and said they were going off in the big boat to look for him.

'Jesus help us! So they must have started home.'

'Yes,' said Klávus, 'but remember that every corner of this vale of misery is in God's keeping, and the Lamb has given His angels charge to guide them to the Rock of Salvation somewhere on the way home. God is good, and holds His protecting hand over all them that have the Seal of Life on their brows.' He invited her to come back with him, and not sit there alone in the house sorrowing.

'Yes, I think I will come over with you. It's always a consolation to be with other people.' She picked up her knitting and put out the lamp.

But at the same moment Klávus caught her round the waist and gave her a hug, went all soft-tongued and wanted to kiss her. But she bit him so hard that he shrieked and ran for the door. 'Shame on you, you old beast, not leaving an old woman like me alone,' she shouted. She lit the lamp again, and sat down by the fireside with her knitting.

Ketil lay in the boathouse, struggling not to fall asleep. He thought it would be keeping poor faith with his friend if he were unable to watch over him one night through. But he was an old man, and tired out, so that now he had a little peace, and was once again warm, he began to feel sleepy. And the waterfall foamed on in a very sleepy way. He closed his eyes, thinking, 'The body is under cover, and He who is mightier than I is surely keeping watch here tonight. So perhaps it's all the same if I do doze off.' So he slept.

A little later his sons, clad in oilskins and sea boots, came clattering into the boathouse. The first one had a pressure lamp in his hand, which he set down on the boat. He looked down into the stern and said, 'Some of this boat's crew won't be pulling an oar again.'

Then Ketil got up out of the straw.

'What's happened to you?' asked the sons. 'And where's Kálvur?'

'He's all right, he's lying here asleep.'

'Oh yes, it could have been a lot worse.'

They gave them some food, and scalding hot coffee-and-spirits, helped them into dry clothes, and took them on board. Lias Berint they wrapped in a sailcloth and carried to the shore. But then came the skipper who had married his niece, in another boat. So he took the body home with him.

When they landed, Ketil said, 'God be thanked we have reached the village again. The journey could have gone better, but it was doubtless God's will that it should have been thus.'

'You should be pleased you've got back with a whole boat and all your straw,' said his sons. 'As for Lias Berint, he's well out of it. He's had a lifetime of grinding toil, and now he's shed the burden.'

'Still, it's a hard thing to lose your life.'

'Not for a worn-out fellow like that,' answered the sons.

'Well now, in the old days that would have been thought slanderous talk, but things are so much altered nowadays – I don't know.' And Ketil and Kálvur went to their house.

'How's it going with the measles?' they asked as they came in through the door.

Ketil's wife beamed at them. 'Bless you, there's no measles in the village. One of the pastor's children got a two-oyru piece stuck in his throat, that's why the doctor came.'

Then Kálvur had to laugh, because he thought it a bit stingy of the pastor to fetch the doctor just to rescue a two-oyru piece.

The following day, Ketil began thatching, but he reflected that if this talk about the measles had not arisen, they would have stayed at home, Lias Berint would perhaps still be alive, and they themselves would probably have made do with the roof as it was, until the next spring.

CHAPTER NINE

Ketil got up before sunrise, raked together the embers of the peat fire, and put some water on to boil. Then he went outside, opened up his codpiece, and looked up into the sky. 'Fine weather this morning,' he said to Klávus, who stood outside his house on a similar errand. 'Yes indeed,' said Klávus, 'a blessed gift from the Lord. Praise be to God, who every morning makes the sun rise on the repentant and the unrepentant sinner.'

'This northerly wind is sharp, so if it holds, we should have a few days of good weather,' said a third old man. They could not see him, but could hear the splash of water in the dark.

Then Tummas came along in search of news, shining his pocket torch.

'Damn the fellow, coming snooping around,' snorted the old men, buttoning up their breeches. 'Nowadays you can't even pass water in peace at this time in the morning.'

Tummas laughed and said that folk didn't do this sort of thing in public any more.

'No, I suppose not – everything's got to be so classy nowadays.'

'What are you folk doing today?' asked Tummas; but the old men would not answer. 'You're not going to pick up any tattle from us,' they said.

Tummas laughed and went on his way. He could still get his news even if they didn't say anything; he could guess.

When Ketil went back into the kitchen, one of the hens muted on him. 'Damn you!' he cried, and grabbed up to the beam for the hen, seized it, got a stranglehold on it and was about to wring its neck; but then he thought better of it and flung it into the byre instead.

When the water was boiling, he took his wife and son some sweet tea in bed. Today they were going to Lias Berint's funeral, so they had to be very early on their way.

Ketil's wife asked what the weather was like.

'Very good weather for crossing the hills – a sprinkling of snow, and the ground hard underfoot.'

The old woman thought it would be best to slip out of the village before folk were about, so that they wouldn't be so spied on.

Ketil thought so as well, and went to feed the cow. As he stepped into the byre he trod on the hen and squashed it flat.

'You always blunder about the place when you first get up, don't you?' mocked his wife.

Ketil was annoyed at himself for what he had done, and tried to get the hen to stand up, but it couldn't lift its head. So he had to wring its neck.

'Don't throw it on the muck heap,' said the old woman. 'Let the pastor have it.'

'Why can't we eat it ourselves?' said Kálvur. 'Give it to me.'

'No, so help me, nobody in this house is going to eat it,' said the old woman. 'You're not having it – it would make you perpetually ravenous.'

'What's ravenous, mother?'

'That's when you can never be filled.'

'Why won't it make the pastor ravenous?'

'I don't know how it is with the pastor. Those Danes eat anything and everything.'

Kálvur also got out of bed. He was not going with them, but was to help them to get ready. He was upset not to be going with them to the funeral, but the old folk told him that if he came he would have to lay his hand on the body to take his last farewell, and that he would not dare to do when so many strangers were present.

'Go and fetch my black leather shoes that stand under my bunk,' said Ketil to his son.

Kálvur returned with them. 'Father,' he said, 'they're ever so mouldy. Shall I pluck them?'

'Don't talk nonsense, you chump! Pluck a pair of shoes? Whoever heard of such a thing? Take a rag and polish them.'

The old woman had decked herself like a bride. She had on a fine collar standing up as high as her ears, puffed sleeves, so slim a waist as to look truly remarkable, a towering hair-style and a headscarf bound right behind it. Kálvur was speechless. 'Mother can be as fine as this when she really wants to be!' he thought.

When they were ready to go, day was just dawning. 'God be with you, my lad,' they said to Kálvur. 'Behave yourself, look after the house, feed the hens, give the cow some water, and don't let the cat get into the storehouse. We'll be back about sunset.'

Kálvur stood looking at them for a time. When they were out of sight, he threw out his chest and spat right into the yard. 'Now I'm king of the castle,' he said to Klávus's daughter, who had come outside with the ashes. 'Now we can really do some courting.'

'What's that?'

'I'm in the house on my own.'

She threw down the ashes, and they both went inside.

When the old people reached the wall, Ketil's wife hitched up her skirt, and took off her headscarf. She turned around to look at the village, and said, 'It's forty years, in Jesus's name, since I was last in another village.'

'It's a long time. The young folk are always going away,' said Ketil.

'The young folk, yes. God never sends us a day but the post boat's full of them. I can't imagine what they can be about every time.'

'They haven't so very much to do, I think; but what annoys me is how they can bring themselves to spend good money on all this gadding about – and where do they get the money from?'

'Yes, because they're always bellowing that they haven't enough, and if they go to the shop, they have to have credit.'

'I don't know how the world's got this way. The older folk scraped and struggled every day, and tried to get good value out of every penny, and there was nothing to spare. You were reckoned to have done well if you gave every man his due. But now! The young folk spend their working days the whole year round in idle amusement. But they seem to get by somehow.'

'Yes, yes,' said the old woman, 'they get by, to be sure. But it's not the way now that it used to be. Nowadays, the folk who are in debt hold their heads as high as everyone else.'

Then, for the first time, they saw the sun, shining through a mountain pass on the neighbouring island of Streymoy. The wet black basalt cliff lines glittered, the hillside pasture slopes shone yellow, and the dark gullies took on a blue tinge. They heard a shepherd somewhere or other, calling out his long 'Hooh, hooh,' and they heard the clink of his staff on the rocks as he made his way to the bleating sheep below him.

Later, Ketil said quietly, 'I feel bad about it, that Lias Berint should have died when he was on a journey with me, but it was just as much his errand we were on as my own, and I know very well that I was no cause of his death.'

'You've nothing to reproach yourself for,' replied his wife. 'But the people he was living with should feel a good deal worse, for if anyone did cause his death, they did. And yet, I don't know. No one leaves this world before his time is up. And when a man has reached the end of his time, fate will always find a way. How did the skipper look that night?'

'I don't know, we didn't talk a great deal, but I thought he seemed very sad.'

'Was the body knocked about much?'

'Not a lot. There was a wound in the head, and that was all. I got a little blood on me while we were carrying him. But he's happy enough now, and not likely to come back for anything. The property of his that he left in our house, I shall give to the skipper. Then I shall have been as upright as it was in my power to be.'

'Did he leave anything with us?'

'There were just those piltocks and a piece of wood he found that day.'

When they came in sight of Lias Berint's village, the old woman was quite overwhelmed. 'Lord bless us, it's a completely different village from what it was forty years ago.' She saw the good old houses standing askew and looking quite wretched amid all the new ones. And there wasn't a muck or ash heap in sight.

Under the gable end of what used to be the finest farmhouse in the village, they met a wrinkled old man whom they knew. 'Good day,' they said.

'Good day,' snorted the old man.

'You can't recognise this village again, there's been so much new building,' said the old woman.

'You may well say that,' the old man replied, wrapping his coat tighter round him, and shivering.

'Whoever manages to pay for all this?' asked Ketil's wife.

'The sea, missus, the sea pays.'

'Who lives over there?' The old woman pointed to a newly-painted house.

'You may well ask. An old farm hand of mine who went to sea ... And here I am, ugh!'

'Didn't you have a son?'

'He's got a new house just the same way as the others.' The old man snorted and went in.

It was so early in the day when Ketil and his wife came to the skipper's house that nobody else had arrived. 'We weren't altogether happy about Lias Berint coming to us,' said Ketil, 'because you might think we had enticed him into leaving you ...'

'No, don't be silly, we don't think any such thing. It was very good of you to take him in with you that time.' The skipper invited them into the parlour. 'Please sit down in here. I'll come back after a bit, but there's a good deal to look after on a day like this.'

The old couple stood there amazed, everything was so fine. They made themselves as slim as possible, and both sat on one chair, so as not to disarrange more of the furniture than was necessary. When they were sitting down Ketil asked his wife, 'Would you like to have all the things that are in here?'

'I don't know. For our own use I wouldn't strain myself to have them, but it would perhaps be rather nice when there were visitors.'

'Perhaps,' said Ketil. 'No, I don't think I'd want to change. I wouldn't be at my ease in the middle of all this lot. If I had money, I'd rather save it, or buy a guilder of land with it.'

Then a man flung the door open, and introduced himself as Jensen.

Jensen was the only man in the village who was known by his surname. In his younger days he had spent a whole year in Copenhagen. There he had learnt to express himself in high-flown terms, to wear a collar, and to gossip about every morsel of food he found himself confronted with. People were filled with admiration, elected him to every possible position, and he was invited to be godfather in every house in the village. Mothers tried to fling their daughters into his arms; but he married the midwife, and she was from another village. Now the fellow was chairman of the parish council, and had ten lesser positions as well. Besides this, he was sub-postmaster and supervisor of the telephone exchange. However, from his Danish period there now remained only his affected way of mixing Danish words in with his Faroese when he was speaking. The collar, that symbol of his social pretensions, disappeared at the time he embezzled from the district treasury. Then folk felt sorry for him, and to mollify him elected him auditor of the village Medical Insurance Fund and chairman of the Bull Cooperative. He had illegitimate children all around the place, but they were all thriving very nicely, God be praised.

'A melancholy occurrence, this of Lias Berint,' he said to Ketil and his wife. 'It is much to be deplored that he should have been so infelicitous as to lose his life on that seacoast.'

'Yes, it was,' answered Ketil, too shy to say any more. He thought how little he and his family could measure up to this man who had been in Denmark.

'Lias Berint was a man of remarkable commercial rectitude,' continued Jensen. 'I can assure you, he is one of the few deceased of this village who have not been in arrears, either for rates, medical insurance premium or bull maintenance subscription. My position in the community is of such a character as to afford me an intimate insight into numerous circumstances of a personal nature, with which people in general are not acquainted.'

'Yes, indeed,' said Ketil and his wife. They longed to be back home again – it was so embarrassing to be in this position.

Then the schoolmaster came in, slow on his feet, but remarkably nimble in his wits. He sat down and looked about him.

Jensen went over to him to talk about the melancholy occurrence, the infelicitous circumstances and the special character of his position in the community.

But the schoolmaster started to laugh. 'Cut it out, Jensen, and talk like a human being. If you must talk in Danish, then do it in proper Danish and not in that hotchpotch.'

The old folk nodded at each other. They had been sitting there afraid of seeming ridiculous, but now they saw that it was Jensen who was ridiculous. They were very grateful to the schoolmaster.

'A man who has been abroad,' said Jensen, trying to defend himself, 'is bound to be exposed to the influences of a foreign culture.'

'An unfortunate journey it was for you,' teased the school-master, 'when you came home as a two per cent Dane.'

Jensen tried to counter the schoolmaster's quips, but he always got the worst of it. Finally, Jensen leaped at him and they started struggling in the parlour, until the pastor came in, dressed in cassock and collar. Then they remembered that it was a funeral they had come to, and stopped.

They went to church with the coffin. The pastor stepped forward to the chancel steps to give his sermon. Lias Berint had been an excellent man, he said, but he had been so modest, that no one had noticed his excellence, and he had received few of the good things of this life. But now he had received his reward, and this, neither moth nor rust would corrupt. God had been so merciful to Lias Berint as to withhold from him the things of this life, to reward him so much the more in the heavenly kingdom.

Tears filled the eyes of the older people, but the younger ones smiled.

It was a fair step from the church to the graveyard. In the front of the procession they were singing hymns, but there was a good deal of fussing and whispering through the crowd at the back, all chattering about how Jensen and the schoolmaster had come to blows. The old men only wanted to know who had had the better of it, but the womenfolk were shocked; fighting at a funeral, whoever heard of such a thing? If it hadn't been such a good man as Lias Berint who had died, his spirit would surely have walked.

But some laughed. 'What fine fellows our pillars of society are!' they said. 'He'll have to be elected to something else now. The time he stole from the district treasury, you made him an auditor. Now he's shown himself to be a man of violence, he's sure to be made a deacon and a parochial church councillor.'

'The schoolmaster was just as bad.'

'No, the schoolmaster couldn't help Jensen leaping at him.'

The graveyard was a mass of withered angelica, docks and nettles. The crowd trampled its way through the wilderness to the graveside. The grave-digger was running about between the graves with his spade over his head, chasing a foal that had strayed in through a hole in the fence. The old men shook their sticks and grumbled about this desecration. 'A man can't lie in his grave now without the risk of having his legs broken!' 'Whose fault is it?'

'It's Jensen who's churchwarden.'

When they got back to the skipper's house, Klávus was sitting there eating, with his top trouser button undone, and a forehead bathed in sweat. 'Jesus be praised,' he said, 'for the Lord has opened His gate for Lias Berint. Blessed is he who has entered the New Jerusalem and can refresh himself in Abraham's bosom. But sinner, you who wander back into the wilderness, despair not, but turn to the Lord, for behold, the Kingdom of Heaven is at hand, and the Prince has sent out His servants to bid both the halt and the blind to the blessings of His marriage feast. Thank you, thank you, skipper, for refreshing my body at your table; but if you should have a morsel of food with which to console a humble servant of the Lord on his perilous way back to his lowly home, then your reward will be double on that day.'

'Gladly,' said the skipper. 'Certainly you can have a bite with you for the road.'

'A blessing on you for that! If you in the purity of your heart will look down on the needy wretch and provide him with sustenance, I can find something to put it in.' And Klávus took a sack out of his sealskin bag.

But when Ketil and his wife arrived, Klávus took himself off.

They sat down to eat. Lias Berint's niece came to them, and sat down to talk.

'Well, I don't know,' she said of Lias Berint, 'old people are so odd. He'd been living in a hovel, but the people he was living with died, so we had to take him in here. We could see right away that he wasn't happy, and longed to be away. Neither the board nor the lodging suited him. But all the same, we tried to be patient with him – though we couldn't allow him to spit in his bedroom, or go into the parlour with his wooden shoes on. That was why my husband tried to get him his old-age pension, and thought also of building him a cabin, so that he could live on his own. That was why he left us. How did you manage with him?' she asked Ketil's wife, but just then a girl came and called the niece away, so Ketil's wife managed to avoid giving a reply.

'It would be best if we slipped off right away,' said the old folk to each other. They felt themselves strangers here, and they felt unable to measure themselves against any of the people they were meeting. Even to eat was a trial for them, because it was not the same as sitting at home with their own familiar wooden dish. Not until they had passed the infield wall, and changed their shoes, away from other folk, did they feel safe and happy once again. They had brought a bit of food with them from home, and now they ate it and went on again.

Evening was beginning to close in.

As the day wore on, Ketil's eldest son said to his wife, 'Just slip over to the old folk's place now it's getting late, and put their supper on the boil for when they come back, poor things. They could easily come over and have supper with us, but I know they wouldn't want to – old people are like that.'

His wife went over. When she reached the house, Kálvur and Klávus's daughter were in the old couple's bunk together locked in each others' arms, and fast asleep. She shrieked out, and ripped the bedclothes from them. They leapt out in great confusion, and disappeared.

When the old folk returned, the house was warm, everything was tidy, and supper was ready.

'Ah, it's grand to come back to a house like this,' said Ketil. His wife thought so too, but when she saw that her daughter-in-law was sitting by the fire knitting, she did not answer him.

The daughter-in-law put up her knitting. 'I thought I'd heat you up a bit of supper for when you came back,' she said. Then she went.

Ketil's wife said, 'I suppose it was wrong of me not to thank her.'

'Yes,' said Ketil, 'I think you were being a bit pig-headed. It would not have been pleasant coming back to a cold house.'

'Yes, true enough, but I think I'd rather come back to an empty grate than stand under an obligation to my daughter-in-law.'

'That's wrong of you,' said Ketil. He was quiet for a time, and then went on in a subdued tone, 'Do you think it is right before God to be like that?' The words came out reluctantly, for he felt that one should store these things in one's heart, not have them on one's lips.

His wife tipped the water from the pot and began to serve the supper.

Then their eldest son came in, chuckling. 'Is Kálvur in?' he asked.

'No, he's not been here since we came back, but he must be somewhere around. Did you want him?' said Ketil.

'Oh, no, I don't want him, but he and Klávus's daughter were lying in your bed together when my wife came in this evening. Now I suppose he's all bashful and gone and hidden himself away somewhere. I'll go and have a look for him.'

Ketil's wife began to weep, while Ketil sucked his beard into his mouth, and sat with his elbows on his knees, chewing it. Everything around him seemed to stand still. Their supper was steaming away in front of them, but they did not see it. A belated hen tried to fly up to the beam, but fell back time and again, but they didn't notice that. The old couple could not bear hearing that Kálvur had slept with Klávus's daughter, for they were certainly not married. They had heard of such things happening in foreign parts, and maybe in Tórshavn and Tvøroyri, but that such people could be here in their own village they would never have imagined. And now their own son was one of them.

Then they heard a voice outside, and the eldest son came in again, still chuckling, and holding Kálvur by the shoulders and pushing him in front. 'Look, here he is – I found him in the hay.'

Kálvur was crying and dabbing at his eyes. His hair was full of hay, and he had lost one of his wooden shoes.

The old folk sat there like statues, neither looking up nor speaking.

Kálvur sat on the bench snivelling. His brother gripped his shoulder and said, 'Don't sit there crying, lad; you're a grown man. I'm not going to do anything to you. I just wanted you indoors before night came on.'

'Yes, but what if the Devil should come for me?'

'Oh, shut up, Kálvur, the Devil's not bothered about what you and Klávus's daughter were up to. But you must face your responsibilities – you must marry her.'

But Kálvur said that he could never bring himself to face the pastor.

'Don't fret about that, I'll come with you,' said his brother, laughing fit to burst.

'I don't see that this is a laughing matter,' said Ketil.

'You should rather weep, the shame he's brought on the household.'

'No, there's nothing to weep about,' replied his son. 'What shame is there if Kálvur does have an urge for a woman? I'm pleased he's got that much manhood in him.' And then he went.

Heavy of heart, Ketil set about burning Lias Berint's bed-straw. He consoled himself with the idea that the Lord might perhaps be merciful to Kálvur, since he had given him so little understanding.

CHAPTER TEN

Christmas was approaching, and it was not fishing weather. Spirits steadily sank in Ketil's house. The old folk racked their brains night and day for ways of laying their hands on a few pence, for an announcement had been posted on the notice board that the District Sheriff would be coming to the village early in the new year, and that the whale-meat bills would be paid then. But they saw no way through. And the cow had not calved, although she was overdue. The old woman tried giving her warm water, but still no calf came. They had wool to spin and knit up, but there was so little time left that this work would not meet their needs.

One Friday morning the church bell rang, the signal that Holy Communion would be celebrated the following Sunday. Ketil and his wife resolved to take communion, although it was not their turn. They did not talk about why they should go again this time, but this had happened many times before in their lives, when difficulties had been at their greatest.

On Saturday, Ketil came back from the fields earlier than usual, and neither of them worked that evening. On Sunday morning, they had a cup of tea when they got up, but ate nothing. Long before service-time they were sitting in their Sunday clothes, ready to go off. Ketil stepped in and out of the courtyard to see whether people were on their way to church, for it could always happen that they might miss the bell.

Once when Ketil was in the yard, Tummas went by. He said nothing, and did not stop, but he told the people in the house next door that Ketil was standing by his door, dressed ready for church. 'Didn't they take communion last time the pastor held service here?' he asked.

'Yes,' replied Ketil's neighbours, 'they did. But Ketil's family always have to be different from everyone else. What other reason could they have for breaking the old custom?'

'That I don't know,' said Tummas. 'Remorse, maybe?'

'Why should they feel remorse more than we or anyone else?'

'I don't know, but I just heard that some folk think it a bit odd that anyone should fall and kill himself in a fairly flat place.' Tummas said this from the doorway, as he was on the way out.

Ketil's neighbours gaped and goggled. 'No, this must be evil tongues telling such a story. Ketil could never be so wicked as to wish any harm on Lias Berint.'

'No, you'd think not; but you can't be sure. They could have been drunk, or they could have quarrelled about land. People said when Lias Berint came to live with Ketil that land was at the back of it.' This idea upset them so much that they had to go out and talk it over a bit more.

When they got outside, they met people from other houses Tummas had visited, and they learned in addition that Lias

154

Berint's title deeds had been in the boat. Klávus brought that information back to the village the day he had been to the funeral. Now people began to make free with their guesses. Gracious heavens, what news for a Sabbath morning! Women, half-dressed, and their hair streaming behind them, ran from house to house. 'Jesus help us, have you heard ...?' 'Yes, too true I've heard about it, but do you know anything else?' 'Oh yes, now they're saying ...' And the story grew with the telling.

Two elderly spinsters ran from one part of the village to another, their pattens in their hands for speed, darting breathlessly into people's houses with the news. 'Now they're saying that Ketil did away with Lias Berint that day! Yes, because why else should he fall and kill himself on level ground near Oyragjógv? Just to get his title deeds from him. There were ten title deeds in the boat, according to what Klávus told Tummas. And now his wife's dragging him to the communion service today. They say he's quite beside himself with remorse, and doesn't look like a human being any longer. Oh, my dear, you've no idea how upset we are about this. Of course we don't believe a word of it – it's just evil talk.'

The church bell rang, and Ketil and his wife set out. They had a smelling-bottle which they passed to each other – it was a great help if you felt ill in church. They walked slowly and silently; he went first and she followed. They were surprised to see so many people afoot that day, but they thought no more of it. In the dimness of the porch, they took another sniff at their bottle, before going to their usual places.

The church was full. A mass of folk who were not usually to be seen there, crowded the gallery and the porch, waiting to catch sight of Ketil, who was supposed to look so ghastly.

Tummas sat in the gallery, chewing tobacco and spitting into the eaves. He was rather uneasy, feeling uncertain how all this was going to end.

The two old spinsters sat stretching their necks and looking at the door, trying to look shocked. Their eyes were agoggle and their lips pursed.

When Ketil and his wife stepped into the aisle, he went first, his hands together and his head bowed, quietly and with a peaceful expression. His wife followed, a little bent, like all women when they take communion, holding her shawl round her as she always did in church. A whisper went round the congregation, 'They look just as they always do!'

Then everyone changed their minds: 'No, of course not, a murderer doesn't look like that. Shame on the man who spreads such slanders! He ought to be soundly punished for weaving together such a tissue of lies.'

Tummas tried to efface himself. 'I said nothing. They've no cause to blame me,' he told himself. He saw the stern glances that people were giving him, and a young man came up and kicked him hard on the shins with his boot.

The old spinsters tried so hard to diminish their height that their Adam's apples slipped right down below their blouse collars. 'No, we said all the time it was just evil talk that people had put together – as if anybody could bring themselves to do a thing like that,' they told themselves.

Ketil and his wife went up to the altar, for this was the nearest approach they could make to God Himself. They would try this last way to get the whale-meat bill paid – by praying in front of the very altar.

When people came back from church, the whole village

was in turmoil. The story about Ketil had come to the hearing of people from other villages who were in the place, and it had been telephoned all round the island and outside it. 'The whole thing's a lie,' said the people who had been in church. 'We could tell by the way they looked.'

The reaction was violent. The villagers wanted to get at the people who had peddled around such slanders. The village lads caught one of the old spinsters outside the churchyard wall, tied her skirt up over her head, and painted her backside red. She had to bite a hole in her skirt to get free again.

Towards bedtime, Tummas came wandering through the village. Ketil's eldest son fell in with him. 'Now, Tummas,' he said, 'have you heard any news?'

'No, I don't know any. Wind looks like freshening northerly again.'

'Well, well, you don't know any news. I heard you'd been accusing my father of manslaughter – surely that must be big news?'

'I never said that.'

'No, I suppose not.' Ketil's son now gripped him by the shirt front, flung him down into a muddy puddle in the middle of the lane, and gave him a sound drubbing. 'Next time you slander anyone, you'll get your jaw broken,' said Ketil's son. Then he thrust him away.

When he got home, he told his wife about what he had done, and laughed about it.

'You can't be right in the head,' said his wife nervously, 'laying hands on the man. Why didn't you report him?'

'Why didn't I report him? What the hell's the use of that?

Just to let the court squeeze money out of him? And in the meantime his wife and children would go hungry.'

The next day was good fishing weather, and Ketil and Kálvur went out with the boat, but caught nothing. The second and third day they also caught nothing they could sell. The fourth day, when Ketil's middlemost son came down to help them get their catch ashore, he saw nothing in the boat but two small cod, and said, 'It's a shame the sea's so damned empty.'

Ketil answered gently, 'No, my lad, it's not damned empty, but blessedly empty.' And he went home with eyes glazed and head hung.

'How did it go with you today, did you catch any fish?' asked his wife with a trembling voice.

'No, we didn't catch a thing. We've tried so thoroughly now, that I think there's no use trying again even if it should be good weather tomorrow.'

They went to bed early that evening, but the old couple could not sleep, but lay silently, each deep in thought.

Some way through the night, Ketil said to his wife, 'You're not asleep, are you?'

'No.'

He had heard her crying. An hour later, he spoke to her again. 'It doesn't do any good crying, old girl.'

'We'll be sold up,' she whimpered.

'Yes, we will for sure ... But it's God's will, and it must be done.' They talked no more that night.

The next morning their cow started to calve. Now this would hardly help the whale-meat bill much, because it would be too short a time to fatten up the calf, but it was some consolation all the same.

Ketil sat at the end of the bench by the door so that he could look at the cow through the peephole. His wife stood by the fireplace, heating up water. Kálvur stood by the door with the bolt in his hand, looking though the latchhole into the yard. If Klávus came, he was to bolt the door. They didn't want him about while the cow was calving, for he always brought them bad luck.

While they were sitting there, Ketil's eldest son came in to borrow a creel. He began to laugh, remembering these customs from his youth. He took Kálvur away from the door and held him. 'Haven't you given up all this business yet? It's only silly superstition,' he said.

'When you *know* that Klávus brings bad luck,' said his mother, 'it's no superstition then.'

'But do you know that he's ever done any harm?'

'Yes, he's been in the house twice when our cow has been calving, and things went wrong both times. The first time the calf died, and the second time the cow milked blood.'

'Yes, but what of that? Are things like that so very uncommon? It would have happened just the same even if Klávus had not been there.'

'No, I don't think so,' replied Ketil. 'Why should it be remarkable for Klávus to bring bad luck on occasions like this? A man who always treads in unlawful paths will bring no good with him, that we may be sure of.'

'That's just silly talk,' said the son. 'I'll go straight over to Klávus's, and ask him to come over, and then you'll see whether anything happens.'

'No, no, please, son, you must do no such thing – we couldn't bear to lose this calf!' said the old woman.

'All right, I was only teasing. Nowadays we treat this sort of thing rather as a joke.' He went off with the creel.

'I can't understand that man,' said Ketil's wife, 'how he can be so cheerful all the time, a man who's got a house full of unpaid bills, while we're so worried about a single one.'

Later in the day the cow dropped her calf, and Ketil's wife gave her a good milking. 'God be praised that everything's gone so well,' said the old folk.

Kálvur had practically lost his voice since his sin. The old folk had to console him, and tell him he must not lose heart, though he must not do such a thing again.

He promised that he wouldn't.

But one day they went to the rectory with him to have the banns entered. Then he recovered his voice, and asked whether it was still a sin to sleep with his girl.

'Oh yes, definitely, right until I say to you, "Be fruitful and multiply",' answered the pastor.

The next morning Ketil felt rather poorly, but he got up all the same.

'You ought to be lying quietly in your bed. There's nothing to be earned anyway,' said his wife.

'Maybe so, but I thought I'd go along to the pastor for leave to go onto the bird cliffs.'

'Onto the bird cliffs!' said his wife, astonished.

'Yes, maybe I could net some fulmars. If we sold them, it would help quite a bit.'

'I wouldn't dare to let you go – you're so old, your legs are almost dead underneath you.'

He thought that was no objection. So he went to the rectory.

When he got there, the pastor was arguing with a man about land. 'You won't be renting any of my infield again,' he said. 'The hay you gave me as rent last autumn was quite useless.'

The man blamed the dry weather. 'If I can't have any of your infield again, I'll have to kill the cow.'

'You've deserved no better, because there's always trouble with you. But you're not the only one; nowadays it seems to be just the same whatever I do, I get blamed regardless. But remember this, it doesn't pay to set yourself against me, because I own both the infield and the turbary in this village, and without my leave, you'll get neither milk nor fuel.'

'I thought a priest was supposed to be a merciful man.'

'Yes, that's just it,' answered the pastor sharply. 'I'm a priest, and so I have to put up with anything and everything. But let me tell you this. You give me what is my due, and ask me decently for what you need, and be thankful for what you receive. That is how it should be between Christian folk.'

Another man stood waiting. Now he asked if the other would be much longer.

'No,' said the pastor, and asked him what he wanted.

'Mother asked if you would come over and give her absolution – she's at her last.'

Yes, he would come.

Then Ketil came with his errand.

'Yes, Ketil, you have my leave to go on the bird cliffs, and may Christ be with you. You are a man of the old school, a modest and peaceful man, thankful for the things you have received. But these younger folk, who boast of their right to the land and just about want to seize it for themselves, they don't need to expect any mild treatment from me. For the land and the power in this place are mine.'

So Ketil trudged off with his fowling net. He did not want Kálvur with him, as they owned only one net. He could have had him sitting there ready to carry the fulmars home, but he thought it would be too presumptuous in the sight of God to have a man waiting to carry home birds that were still flying across the cliff face.

Quietly, he walked northwards over the hills, and quietly he sat down by a boulder at the end of the cliff line, and crossed himself. As he traversed the cliffs, his lips were quivering the whole time. He heard stones fall, and lumps of ice detach themselves, but he was not afraid, for these things fell where they were destined to fall, and were guided by a Hand that had the power to steer them.

A short way along the sea cliff he came to a little shelter, where he sat down. The fulmars came, and he swung his net and caught three of them. The fourth time he lifted it, a stone fell from the edge of the cliff above him, and snapped the pole of his fowling net. Of the ten feet of its length, only a stump of three or four feet was left in his hands. It seemed to him as though God Himself had smitten off his hand; he bowed his head and gave God thanks: 'I have deserved no better,' he said. Then he went home with the three birds.

His wife could hardly bear to look at him when he came home, he looked so downcast. He put the stump on the beams, hung the fulmars on a nail the other side of the byre door, and sat down to change his stockings.

Kálvur was not at home.

'I can't do anything more about that whale-meat bill,' he told his wife. 'I don't see any way through now.'

'I understand, my dear,' said his wife, seating herself by the fireplace. 'I'm more troubled for your sake than for the shame of it, and I grudge those people who wish us ill the pleasure of seeing the District Sheriff in the house.'

'I don't know,' said Ketil, 'but I would never dare to look folk in the eye again, if the District Sheriff came in to distrain on us. Have you counted up the bit of money we have?'

'That's soon done.' They went into the bedroom and locked the door, and the old woman fetched out a little box from under the bed. From one of its compartments she took out some crumpled notes and a little small change, slightly over a hundred kroner altogether. They sat silent on the edge of the bed for a time, staring at the little heap.

Then the old woman said, 'I think we'll have to sell the cow.' She looked away and silently wept.

Ketil blanched and felt a singing in his ears. 'That would be like losing one's right hand. She's the only living creature we've got, and we'd be without milk for two years.'

They both went out again, opened the byre door, and stood there looking at their cow. She lay there so clean and beautiful on her bedding, chewing the cud. Ketil hid his face in his hat, while the old woman buried her eyes in his chest.

Before anyone was afoot the next morning, Ketil and Kálvur left the house, taking their cow with them.

ABOUT THE AUTHOR

Heðin Brú (1901–87) – pronounced (approximately) as *Hay-in Broo* – was a native of the tiny village of Skálavík, near the eastern extremity of Sandoy. As a boy he grew up in a community of peasant-fishermen whose way of life had changed little since the Faroe Islands were first settled in Viking times and Christianised in the eleventh century. The little cluster of grass-rooted farmhouses was surrounded by the cultivated infield – mostly under hay for winter fodder for the cows – and beyond its boundary wall lay the moorland pasture, the outfield, where twice a year all the men of the village would round up the sheep, first for shearing, then for the autumn slaughter. It was a community where money was seldom in use, and not easy to come by. However, a thrifty man would have plenty of fish and lamb carcasses hanging up in his slatted wind-house to dry; and the potatoes from his infield, milk from his cows, and sea-birds caught on the sea-cliffs would ensure that in most years he would not go hungry, even if he had to scrape and struggle to pay his taxes. Heðin Brú's boyhood world, then, was one in which people were producing for their own consumption, instead of what other people might be prepared to give money for.

Then as a young man, Heðin Brú entered a quite different world, as a fisherman on one of the old wooden cutters. The fisherman's year used to be divided into seven or eight months of the most harrowing activity, and then four or five months of idleness, when the weather made it impossible for the cutters to operate, though the open village boats might still carry on an inshore fishery on fine winter days, locating the tiny, but very rich fishing-banks with the help of bearings on the land, which had been passed down from father to son as a most precious fund of knowledge. Heðin Brú's first novel, *Lognbrá* (Mirage), published in 1930, gave an account of the development of a boy in a Faroese village. Its sequel, *Fastatøkur* (Firm Grip), which appeared five years later, recounted the experiences of the hero as a young man on board the cutters.

Feðgar á Ferð (literally Father and Son on the Move), or *The Old Man and His Sons*, was first published in the original Faroese in 1940. In a light-hearted and witty way, *Feðgar á Ferð* illustrates the contrast in economic and moral values between the subsistence economy of the world's past, and the market economy of the world's future. The contrast is perhaps more telling in a Faroese setting than anywhere else in the world, but the theme is a universal one.

Extracted from translator John F. West's introduction to the original edition.